And the Two Shall Become One

Legends of the Romanorum, Volume 2

Mychael Black and Shayne Carmichael

Published by Arian Derwydd Books, LLC, 2024.

Legends of the Romanorum, Book 2

Mael and Cian are back in this sequel to The Prince's Angel! Mael has finally decided to declare Cian his consort, and plans to announce it to his court. While this may cause dissention in the vampire ranks, the two lovers have far worse problems.

A demon summoned by Memnet, a rogue vampire, and dirty deals lead to nothing but trouble, and might even kill the pair if they aren't careful. Add in a forbidden love between Brandon and Mael's alchemist Cornelius, who already knew Brandon was the one man he couldn't have, the return of Selena, a vampire Cian doesn't trust, and a very wily archangel, and Mael and Cian have a recipe for disaster.

Only Cian has Mael's back in the shifting political world of court, which worsens day by day as Mael realizes there's a traitor somewhere in his own court. Through it all, it's the love between Mael and Cian that keeps them going, even when things are at their worst.

Can they survive the murky underworld of the creatures who inhabit the night, or will the forces seeking to tear them apart finally succeed?

Chapter One

"I summon thee, Zalael, to this place and offer thee this body as your vessel."

The cadence of the words echoed within the darkened room lit only by candles. The body on the stone altar was less than an hour old, as his death had been a part of the ritual itself. Several moments passed in silence before any movement became visible. With a great gasp for air, the body on the altar jerked with life. His head turned slowly to face Memnet.

"Who dares summon me?" The creature's voice was low, and the question was more growl than words.

Memnet folded his hands in front of him. The protective circle around him guaranteed he would remain unharmed should Zalael not find favor with his offering or the bargain Memnet wished to strike. "I am Memnet, great Zalael." He bowed his head in respect to the demon. As he looked up, his gaze was calm and steady as he took in the form not far from him.

Zalael sat up slowly and moved each arm and leg in turn. He then turned and slid off the altar to stand against it. It took him a moment to gain a sense of balance, and when he finally did, he looked up at Memnet. "And who is Memnet, that he would dare to wake me?"

Memnet studied the face and form the demon inhabited. He had chosen well. The man he picked had an angelic, innocent beauty, with long, silvery blond hair and deep blue eyes. The body, while muscular, wasn't overly so. At 6'3", Zalael was now a truly magnificent creature.

"I am the man who wishes to set you loose on the world. Other than a few chosen tasks, I will leave you free to do as you wish. That is, if you wish to be freed." Somehow he doubted Zalael would choose the alternative of returning to the Abyss again.

A slow smile spread across the demon's lips. "Free?" He moved away from the altar and began circling Memnet. "And what price do you pay? What do I pay? Freedom comes with a price, and calling me from the void carries one just as steep."

"I pay in blood to keep you here, and the price you pay is the inability to walk in the sunlight." Memnet shrugged slightly, thinking those terms to be fair enough.

"Very well. Why have you called me?"

Memnet smiled slowly. "Because I need your unique talent to disrupt the Romanorum." He'd been highly irritated when his plans with the rogues hadn't come to fruition, and just as annoyed to be minus one Daughter, particularly Selena, who had been his favorite. "Are we agreed to mutually help each other, which also includes leaving me in one piece? I also demand that no harm comes to either me or my family."

Zalael stood before Memnet, his eyes narrowing. "And what do I get out of this?"

"What you get out of it is your freedom. After you've accomplished what I want, I will not return you to the Abyss."

"Then we are in agreement," Zalael said. "What do I face?"

Only after he had Zalael's agreement did Memnet step out of the circle, breaking it. "Nothing you can't handle as it's only vampires, and perhaps a few mortals." He went to one of the wooden tables and picked up a piece of paper. "Their names are listed here."

Zalael took the note and glanced over it, nodding as he read each name silently. When he reached the bottom of the list, every muscle in his body tightened visibly. He shot a dark glare back up at Memnet as his jaw clenched. The note crumpled in his fist.

Memnet leaned against the table, relaxed and distinctly pleased that things were going as he wanted. "Is something wrong?"

"There is a name here I know well. What can you tell me about this Cian Carmichael?"

Vaguely surprised by that, Memnet answered him. "Carmichael is a pain in the ass sorcerer. He was the one who successfully hunted far too many of my rogue vampires. As many times as he's shown up, I'd guarantee there is some kind of alliance between him and the Prince of London."

The note burst into flames in Zalael's hand. "What does he look like?"

"Since I've never met the man, I don't know. Though by all accounts I've received, he is considered extremely good looking, a blond-haired man with blue eyes. He should be easy enough to find."

A dark smile spread slowly across Zalael's thin lips. "I see. And what of Mael Black, and Diocourides? I know the second name, although I cannot place it. Given the proximity of the names to Cian Carmichael, I would imagine they are connected somehow?"

"I have pictures of Black and Diocourides I can show you later. It was Carmichael who rescued Black from my Daughter and killed her. So yes, I assume there is an alliance there. And as far as Diocourides goes, he is the head of the Romanorum and creator of all vampires."

"I would very much like to see this Mael Black. If Cian Carmichael rescued a vampire, there must be a very strong connection between them. I will rid you of these beings, although Carmichael will prove to be a bit more difficult than the others."

Directing a knowing look at the demon, Memnet smirked. A small wound opened at the side of his throat and blood welled from the cut but didn't spill as he paused in front of Zalael. "And you will, Zalael, but it wouldn't do to send you out on an empty stomach, now would it?"

With a blur of motion, Zalael's hand closed around Memnet's neck as Zalael shoved him back against the wall. "Don't fuck with me," the demon snarled. He lowered his head and bit down hard on Memnet's throat, swallowing the blood as it filled his mouth.

Memnet laughed. The pain was nothing to him. As he let Zalael feed, he said, "My, but you like it rough, don't you?"

Zalael pulled abruptly from Memnet's neck and licked his lips. "Don't tempt me. When my freedom is won, I will take whatever I want."

"You can do whatever you wish with that freedom. Only our agreement binds you." Assured that Zalael would not harm him or his line, Memnet really didn't give a damn what the demon did.

"And I will do just that." Zalael turned abruptly. "I will let you know when my work is done." With that, he was gone.

* * *

The last thing Selena Kerr remembered was trying to stop Mael Black from killing her. She'd grabbed the sword and when she backed up against the wall, a warmth had flooded through her that she'd never known before. The next thing she remembered was waking up here. And none of the nitwits near her would tell her a thing, until one had said, "Follow me." After walking down numerous corridors she tried to memorize, they stilled in front of a set of impossibly huge, golden doors.

"Are those things real?" When silence greeted her question, she compressed her lips. "I've died and gone to Hell, haven't I?" Without one clue as to what the hell happened or what was going on, she eyed the doors with a touch of impatience, and the nitwit next to her received the same treatment.

A voice, low and thunderous, sounded from within. "Enter." The doors swung open then, washing the corridor with a white brilliance.

The thunderous nature of that voice made her jump before she frowned. She blinked rapidly when the light nearly blinded her. She had the distinct feeling something was trying to intimidate her, and she refused to allow it—even in death. Slowly, she walked into the room. The room itself, with its walls, columns, and floor made of white marble, was the first thing to hit her. Spotting two thrones of a rich, dark wood, she saw a man sitting on the larger one. The smaller throne was empty. The man at the doors quickly closed them behind Selena, leaving her in the cavernous, white room—alone with him.

As she walked farther in, she took careful note of the man himself. She stilled abruptly, her expression altering to almost an awestruck dumbness. The only movement was her eyes as she took in the sight of him, lingering over the angelic beauty of his form before lifting back to his face. Something felt vaguely familiar, as if she should know him somehow, though she'd never seen him before. Judging by the man's sheer beauty, he had to be Lucifer—even if the white was a bit off.

"Holy shit. I'd heard you were gorgeous, but damn."

Lifting a blond eyebrow in vague amusement, the man stood up and stepped down the dais. Wings unfurled from his back and then relaxed. Their emerald feathers shimmered as he walked. "Welcome," he said with a graceful smile.

She took a few more steps toward him before she stopped. "You make a nice welcoming committee. I take it I did die, but if this is meant to be a punishment, somebody messed up." The temptation to reach out and touch one of those wings was strong, but she managed to restrain the urge.

His smile widened and he reached out for her hand. He took it in his and brought it to his lips, kissing the back gently. "I thank you. Come, please sit."

Frowning, she didn't know quite what to make of the man or the feeling that emanated from him as he held her hand. He waved toward the other throne before turning back to his own. Who was he?

"You did die, Selena, but this is not a punishment. If you remember, a man named Cian Carmichael was with you."

"Yes, I remember him. He was a rather pretty one. Had nice wings."

"Cian Carmichael saw something within you, or you would not be before me now. It is he whom you should thank for a second chance, Selena." His voice was calm but stern. "Do you fear me? Is that why you will not sit beside me?"

"You're not Lucifer, are you? And this isn't Hell." She sat down on the second throne gingerly, half-expecting something to bite her. She really did have the feeling somebody'd screwed up. The man laughed. It was a deep, rich sound that permeated the air and had the ability to settle into a person's soul. She shivered.

"No, this is not Hell. And I am not Lucifer." He leaned over and slipped a hand under her chin, drawing her head up to meet a soul-deep, blue gaze. "And no one screwed up."

Finding herself caught by the sapphire eyes, her own widened in confusion before her thoughts caught up with her. "No, this isn't Heaven. It can't be. I don't belong here." Knowing the kind of life she had led, that would have been a given. "Where am I? And how the hell did I get here?" The man released her chin and stood. He disappeared briefly through a doorway behind Selena's throne and then returned, carrying a length of blue velvet, tied with a silver ribbon. "There are only a handful of beings who can wield what lies within this cloth." He opened the cloth and wrapped his fingers around the hilt of a sword. He held it upright before his face and then lowered his gaze to Selena. "And I am their Prince."

"That's the sword Mael Black gave me as a gift. He should have known better. I wanted the Eye." Wanted was a very mild word; desperately needed it was more like it. "If I'm dead and in Heaven, where does that leave me?" It slowly permeated her brain that she was indeed in Heaven, and for some reason, Cian Carmichael had sent her here.

The man lowered the sword, returning it to the cloth as he spoke. "You are in Heaven, Selena. Cian is one of my highest enforcers on Earth and a close friend." Setting the sword on the step of the dais before his throne, he turned back to look at her. "I am Michael, Prince of Heaven. Something within you called out to Cian, yet it was too late for him to do anything about it. He does not have the ability to stop death. He does, however, have the ability to know a good soul from a foul one. If your soul was truly lost, you wouldn't be here now. He gave you a second chance, Selena."

"Second chance?" Another frown furrowed her brow as she remembered that one moment, what it had felt like when Cian had touched her and offered her something she desperately wanted. She just hadn't understood then, and she still wasn't sure she did. "I remember feeling..." She simply trailed off; there were no words to describe it.

"Yes?" Michael watched her for a moment before leaning over and threading his fingers through her hair, cupping her head gently. He pressed his lips softly to her forehead to remind her.

With the touch of his lips to her skin, Selena closed her eyes, feeling the warmth of that alien peacefulness flow over her. Her body and mind relaxed, and there was something inside her that clung desperately to it. It eased so much of the inner pain that nothing else ever had. Words failed her when she tried to open her mouth to speak.

"Do you remember now?" Michael whispered softly. "I can take the pain away, Selena, but you have to want me to. I will do nothing without hearing from you first. Cian tried to save you, but he was unable to. For that, he has spent some time with a pain of his own—a pain of failure. For an angel, that isn't an easy thing to live with."

An unexpected wetness spilled over her cheeks. Turning her head away, not wanting him to see, she swiped at the tears. "I think I understand now. I've lived with all of that for a very long time, Michael. I want it to go away, to not be a part of me anymore."

Michael cupped her face gently, turning her head back to face him. "Do not hide from me, Selena. If you truly want it gone, then look me in the eye and tell me. A person's eyes tell much more than their words; that is something you will come to understand." He brushed his thumb slowly over her lower lip. "What do you want?"

Her mind focused inward, deeper into her own personal hell, and she knew to be completely free of it was what he was offering her. She stared at him, buried deeply within the darkness that had sought to overwhelm her. "I want you to take it away," she whispered, her voice beginning to break. "You can; I know you can. I felt that. Please help me, Michael."

Michael smiled softly and leaned forward, but instead of pressing his lips to her forehead, he pressed them to her own lips. "Give me your pain, Selena. Release it." Even though his mouth remained closed, he began to draw the pain out of her, slowly, so as not to overwhelm her.

Closing her eyes once again, she heard the soft whisper, beckoning to her. For the first time in her entire existence she just let go of what enslaved her, trusting in Michael. Something she had never done in her life was trust another, and she wasn't sure why she did so now. She felt she knew him, somehow, and in a way she really couldn't comprehend. Michael slipped his fingers through her hair to keep her still and opened his mouth on hers. With the slide of his tongue between her lips, the blackness was forced from her soul. A wash of pure peace swelled through her, filling the void within.

Selena began to tremble in response to the sudden draw that left her empty as it took the darkness. The rush that filled her in its wake made her shudder as it enveloped her mind, restoring her soul. Tears fell down her cheeks unheeded as her mind cried out, clinging in desperation. When the blackness within her had gone, leaving her with a sense of peace, Michael's kiss softened before he pulled away. He wiped away the tears from her cheeks with his fingertips.

Selena remained still. She didn't want him to stop. For the very first time, she felt peace within herself and she wasn't frightened anymore. Her fingers tightened momentarily on his arm as she stared back at him, taking in the gentleness of his expression. She smiled back hesitantly, dropping her hand from his arm.

Michael moved his fingertips softly over her cheek to brush over her lips, barely touching them. His gaze moved slowly from her lips to her eyes, holding her in a soft gaze. "You truly are a beautiful woman, Selena, and your soul belongs to you. Let no one ever take that from you again."

She knew he was seeing her as she once had been, the innocence and trust, before her soul had been stolen from her. Tears still burned her eyes, but didn't fall. "This time I want to keep it." The flit of a thought touched her mind in the realization that if she lost it again, she would lose him as well. More than anything, that thought terrified her, though she didn't know why. In only a few moments, this man—this being—had become the anchor she so desperately needed.

"And know that I would fight to keep you as you are now."

When she heard his voice in her mind, her eyes widened as she took in the words and their meaning. A heartfelt gratitude filled her, leaving her not knowing what to say. "I'm not really sure why I received a second chance, but you've given me hope. Thank you isn't enough for saving me."

He smiled and traced his fingertips down her arm to take her hand in his. He entwined his fingers in hers and seemed to be lost in thought for a moment before speaking. "You were given a second chance because Cian had faith in what he saw within you. It isn't hard to see why."

All of her dealings with others had been forced. That Michael seemed willing to be around her, and even help her, completely amazed Selena. She clasped his hand and glanced at the sword on the steps. "I wanted the Eye of Baal, you know. To get rid of Memnet. I was extremely angry at Black for not getting it for me. Somehow, I think the sword was a better gift, and I'm not so angry anymore."

"It was," Michael said. "Cian knew not to give the Eye to Mael Black, and Cian has been its guardian for some time. You will have to face them both, Selena."

She hadn't thought she would have to return. She gripped his hand tighter as she stared at him in dismay. "I don't have to go back, do I? Can't I talk to Cian here?"

Michael knelt before her, bringing him eye-level with her. "You must go back, Selena. Salvation comes with a price—one of repayment. An old adversary of Cian's has awakened, and not even Mael can protect him. You will be needed."

She studied his face for a moment. Unsure of what she saw in him, it still drew her nonetheless. "Then I will return."

"I will always be with you. No matter where you are, I will be with you. All you have to do is need me."

Tilting her head slightly, Selena rubbed her cheek against his hand. "You're going to be a busy angel. You know that, don't you?"

"I'm never too busy," Michael murmured. He carded his fingers back through her hair, letting the silky strands slip between them.

"You say that now, but wait a few weeks."

"I think it's worth the coming trouble."

Spellbound, she leaned toward him. Something inside her wanted to kiss him, and the feeling itself startled her. She'd never wanted intimacy—not like this. Her lips touched softly to his, clinging to the warmth for a brief moment before she pulled back. Mentally berating herself, she settled back in her seat.

Michael seemed to lose his breath for several seconds. When his eyes opened, a quieter, more subdued desire sparkled with their blue depths. "Do you fear me?"

Puzzled by his question, she shook her head. "No. You wouldn't hurt me. I know that, Michael." "I would never hurt you." He brushed his lips over her forehead, moved down the bridge of her nose, then stopped at her lips. "I would do many things," he whispered, "if you let me. But never would I hurt you." His breath warmed her lips and the tip of his tongue slid slowly across them.

Selena took the words for the reassurance they were meant to be. The sensations ghosting across her lips distracted her terribly. A soft noise, barely a whimper, rose in her throat, and she opened her mouth to him. Michael slipped his tongue in, stroking it across hers briefly, and then broke the kiss. He rested his forehead against hers.

"If you like, I will show you to your room. It will be your own haven, whenever you need it. Know that you are safe here, Selena."

She wanted to respond to him, to let him taste her, and a touch of disappointment flared when the moment was gone. Everything left her confused. "Will I be able to stay here for a few days before I have to go back?"

"Yes, but we cannot wait longer than a week. After that, we must leave." He stood and held out a hand to her.

"We? You are going with me?" She stood as he did, taking his hand.

He pulled her gently up against him, folding his wings around her in a clearly protective gesture. "Yes, for the first meeting with Mael and Cian, I will be going with you. Cian will remember what happened and he has become fiercely protective of Mael Black since. I would not put either of you through that alone."

She wasn't used to anyone wanting to protect her like he seemed to. As he held her, she rested her head against his chest, sighing quietly. The centered, peaceful feeling filled her so easily and she could feel the safety of his wings as they closed around her. "I don't think either of them will be very happy to see me at all. But as you said, I have to return."

Michael kissed her hair, "It is something that must be done," he said. "Cian will not hurt you, and at my word, he will not allow Mael to harm you either. You will be safe. Come. I'll show you to your room."

"That's not quite what I was worried about." Not daring to laugh, she curled her hand to his when his wings released her. "Lead the way, McDuff." If she was sorry that he let her go, it didn't show in her expression. Thankfully.

Chapter Two

Since Mael Black had returned to court after the ordeal with Selena, things had been tense. He didn't miss the looks, the whispers that questioned just what sort of hold Cian Carmichael had over him. Mael wasn't about to delve into the reasons why himself. He eyed Cian, who stood before him, the sorcerer's presence oddly comforting to him, despite the rumors. "Others are asking questions about you, Cian."

Cian lifted a pale eyebrow at him. "Asking about me? Or asking about us?"

Mael shook his head. "No, specifically about you."

"What have they been asking?"

Sav, Mael's lead assassin, looked between the two of them, but remained silent, as did the few others in the throne room. Glancing over at her, Mael nodded his head slightly. Sav turned to face Cian. "Mostly it seems to concern questions in the right and wrong places, as if others are trying to find out how powerful you really are. Quite a few have found themselves roughed up over the matter," Sav said.

Cian looked from Sav to Mael. "Why would the question of my power be an issue?"

"The going rate for information about you ranges up there into a couple of thousand if the info is deemed worth it. Your guess as is good as mine as to why it's worth so much, Sorcerer. You've become quite well-known as a vampire hunter," she said with a shrug.

"Have any of those interested parties been involved in the magical arts?" Cian asked quietly.

"Not so far as I can tell. Most of them seemed to be simple henchmen and not that hard to dispose of. A couple tried to detain me as well. For some reason, they seem to think I knew more about you. Only a certain number knew that I was trailing you before."

Mael stood and restlessly paced the top of the dais. "In my own court?"

"I do not give out my trust freely," Cian said under his breath, but loudly enough for Sav and Mael to hear him. "And there are only a few within this court who have garnered my trust." Cian reached out, grabbing Mael's shoulder to stop him, and pulled him close enough to whisper in his ear. "Only dark magic can harm me, Mael."

Mael relaxed a bit, but he was still angry. "It isn't a matter of a trust, Cian. Someone in my court is stirring things up, but for what purpose?"

Cian looked at Mael for a moment and opened his mouth to respond, but before any words could form, a swirling, red mass of clouds shimmered in the middle of the throne room. Cian's eyes widened considerably. Mael opened the mental connection between them, seeing a look of recognition on Cian's face.

"What is going on?"

"I don't know why he's here, Mael," Cian said aloud. "But as Sav serves you, I serve Him." A tall figure stepped out of the portal then, his emerald wings shifting for a moment before settling against his back. He looked at Cian and smiled.

Both of Mael's brows rose as he took in the sight before them. A complete study in diplomacy, he bowed his head toward the man, assuming this to be the Archangel Michael. "Welcome to my court."

"Thank you, Prince Black," Michael said with a bow of his head. "I have come with purpose: a meeting and a warning."

The moment the woman behind Michael came into view, Cian's wings spread out to their full span, curled over in readiness. He immediately stood directly between Mael and the woman, his stance leaving nothing to the imagination.

Nothing but complete and total casualness was visible in Selena's manner until Cian's display.

"What? None of you have ever seen the walking dead before?"

Cian shot a disbelieving look at Michael. "Why is she here?" Michael raised his hand in a simple gesture, and Cian's wings descended in response. Cian knelt down on one knee, bowing his head in fealty. "Forgive me, my Lord."

Michael slipped a hand under Cian's chin, and Cian stood. "She is here because of your faith, Cian. The darkness within her soul is gone." He looked over at Selena and gave her a wry smile. "Although there isn't much I can do about her personality."

Mael looked over them all, rapidly accessing the situation. He raised his hand and dismissed his court, not wanting witnesses to any more of this. Seeming more than happy, Sav, Jensen, Ben, and Cornelius hastily made their way toward the door and exited the room. Feeling the rush of chaotic thoughts from Cian, Mael stepped closer to him.

"Prince Black, I am relieved to find you well once more. Cian has always been a devoted commander and friend."

Bowing his head slightly, Mael gave Michael a smile as Cian backed up, slipping an arm protectively around his waist. "It is a pleasure to have you in my court, Michael." His smile softened as he felt Cian's arm encircling him. Out of the corner of his eye, however, he watched Selena, little trusting her.

"My faith," Cian said quietly. "I thought I had lost what it was I felt from her."

"No, my friend. What you saw was enough to bring her to me," Michael said. "I have come with a warning. I fear an old 'friend' of yours is waking. I do not know more, other than he has sent others abroad to find out if you are indeed the same one who banished him."

Cian stiffened. "Who?"

Frowning slightly, Selena appeared as if she didn't have the faintest clue what was going on. She stayed silent, though, pressed close to Michael. Michael slipped an arm around her waist, pulling her closer to him. A brow arched in surprise as Mael noticed the almost protective gesture, and a thoughtful furrow etched his brow. When he felt Cian tense beside him, he slid an arm around his lover, distracted by the tenor of his lover's thoughts. A quiet blanket of soothing calm enveloped Cian, giving him as much comfort as Mael could.

"Zalael," Michael answered.

At the mere mention of the name, the color seemed to drain from Cian's face. His arm fell from Mael's waist, and he turned. He began to pace, his wings twitching. Mael stared first at him and then at Michael. The echoes of Cian's thoughts reached him, causing him to frown heavily. "Who in the hell is that?"

"Zalael was one of the first demons I banished after Michael created me. He was also one of the strongest. He knew my secrets, Mael. He knows how to kill me, and succeeded once already. He swore revenge, and I fear he may come to collect that."

Mael moved to his lover, his automatic reaction wanting to erase that look of fear in Cian's eyes. "If it's him, then we'll take care of him, Cian."

"Cian, is there anyone who does not readily like you?" Michael asked.

Cian burst out in a bitter laugh and dropped his head to Mael's shoulder. "Most do not, Michael." He lifted his head to look into Mael's eyes. "If I am in danger, then you most certainly are as well."

Mael slowly combed his fingers through the golden curls of Cian's hair. "It isn't the first time, and it probably won't be the last. We'll deal with it, just like we have everything else."

"We must keep watch," Cian said. "If someone with magical knowledge begins asking questions, then we will know who to start watching closely. Zalael was locked away, deep within the remains of Jericho. If the statue that houses his soul was found by someone with sufficient knowledge, then I am as good as dead."

"Oh, no, not while I'm alive, Cian," Mael said vehemently. "And I will make sure that every resource I have is put to finding out what, if anything, is happening."

"Mael..." Cian sighed as his words trailed off. "If Zalael is indeed waking, then little can be done to keep him from finding me. If someone finds out how to get to my tower, then even it will become unsafe."

"But I think I'm not the only one determined to make sure you and I stay safe." Glancing over at Michael and Selena, Mael watched them briefly. They were talking, standing close enough to bring many questions to mind.

Cian glanced briefly over at Michael and Selena. "Michael trusts her," he said matter-of-factly. "If only for that, I will give her the benefit of a doubt." Cian leaned closer to Mael's face, pinning him with a dark gaze. "But if anyone ever lays another fucking finger on you, I will kill them myself."

"I'm not giving her any benefit of a doubt at this point," Mael said quietly. He had not forgotten the last night he saw her. "But knowing you trust Michael, I'll not say anything."

Cian smiled and slid his arms around Mael's neck. "I trust Michael implicitly; he created me. I've been one of his commanders for some time and just as I would do for you, I would put my own life on the line for him. If he trusts Selena, then there is nothing for me to say." His right wing shifted slightly, brushing the back of Mael's hand. A shudder slid through him.

One of Mael's brows arched, and he briefly caressed a blue feather, just to feel his angel shiver again. "I think you better finish your talk with Michael before other things start coming to my mind."

"Mael, don't do that..." Cian whispered breathlessly. "Not right now..." Chuckling softly, Mael stopped and then stepped back, giving Cian room to breathe.

* * *

"Penny for your thoughts, love?"

Startled by the endearment that had nothing sinister behind it, Selena glanced quickly back up at Michael. "Nobody knows who was really behind all the trouble before. Everyone thought it was me," she said quietly.

Michael turned fully around to hold Selena to him. "If he comes for you, then he will have to go through me first," he whispered gruffly in her ear. His hold around her waist tightened.

Selena shook her head slightly, lost in thought as she slipped her arms around Michael. "I thought he could be behind this. There wasn't a part of anything that happened that he didn't orchestrate, Michael. I played a small part for him. It might be that he is doing this as well." Michael brushed his lips over Selena's forehead softly. "Perhaps you are right. And I would be lying if I said that I do not fear for Cian. He is one of my closest friends. Truth be told, I would be surprised if Memnet is not behind this. Does he have a knowledge of magic? Dark magic?"

Her Father had far more dealings with demons than she ever did. "He dealt in it. Far more than me. The only one I had anything to do with was Sagan. But then, he's rather strange, even for a demon. Memnet was tainted completely." She, on the other hand, only ever asked for information from Sagan. She never asked for power, because she had known how dangerous a route that was.

Michael sighed heavily and rested his cheek on Selena's hair. "Then it is very possible. Although I am glad Cian's finally found someone for him. And I feel I have as well."

Michael had a habit of confusing her all to hell. Fear of her Father only added to the mix of turbulent emotions as Selena clung to the Archangel. His words made her draw back her head, though, to look over at the sorcerer and the prince before her gaze returned to Michael. "I think you're the only one who sees anything worth seeing."

"Perhaps time will change that," Michael said with a smile.

She gave a bit of a laugh because, quite frankly, she couldn't see any worth in herself. It would be highly doubtful if anyone else did either. Even if Michael constantly surprised her with his apparent comfort at being around her.

Michael angled his head down to brush his lips over hers briefly before turning to Cian and Mael. "Cian, there is a possibility of someone to be wary of."

"Who?"

"Memnet."

Cian glared at Mael for a brief moment, his dark gaze reflecting sheer frustration. "Memnet?"

A dark, thunderous look suddenly descended over Mael's face. "How do you know that name?"

Selena merely gave the prince a blank, neutral look as she stepped away from Michael before she answered for him. "Because I gave it to him."

Michael nodded slowly. "It is highly possible that Memnet is behind this. Why he would want Cian dead is beyond me, but Memnet has the power to release Zalael and command him."

Cian slid his hand down to thread his fingers through Mael's. "Who is Memnet and why would he care about me?"

Fury flashed in Mael's dark gaze as it fell on Selena. "You knew where he was, yet you said nothing?"

"He's my Father. What was I supposed to say?"

* * *

It took a moment for Mael to swallow his revulsion and contempt. "Memnet is a foul memory even to our kind. If it's him, he's not after you personally, or even me. He's after Diocourides and the entire Romanorum." Cian's grip tightened considerably on his hand, sending a pulse of soothing light through their connection.

Michael stepped between Selena and Mael. "If that is the case, then his use for one of the strongest and foulest demons is explained. Zalael will gladly assist him, while searching for Cian." He leveled a stern gaze on Mael and then Selena. "You all must work together. I will do what I can, but only Selena and Mael have the immediate knowledge of their society to do what is needed. Cian and I will be forced to deal with Zalael, and ultimately Memnet."

Mael's gaze remained narrowed on Selena. "You are your Father's Daughter."

"Prince Black, Selena: I trust in you both to settle these differences. There is no room for them now," Michael said, sternly but calmly.

Cian pulled Mael back against him. "Calm down, Mael."

Mael knew he had some anger to work out; her hands weren't the only ones he'd suffered at. The hatred was more directed at her Father than her, but she was the only target available. "You have no idea what she has done, or what her Father did." As she stepped out from behind Michael, staring at Mael, Selena's face appeared to be carved in stone. Mael bit back the rest of his words as he forced himself to relax against

Cian. When he spoke again, the words were calm. "I will do what is needed to take care of this."

Michael stepped close to Mael and leaned down to whisper in his ear. "Remember this: Memnet made her into what she was. Direct your anger where it is best served." Mael silently nodded to Michael, though it took considerable effort for him to swallow back his ire. "I must be going. I am leaving Selena here. And to ensure that tempers do not flare out of control, I am leaving Cian in charge. He has been my commander for all of his existence and I trust his judgment above all others."

Cian groaned, but didn't argue. He bowed his head to Michael. "Yes, my Lord."

"I will make sure her accommodations are comfortable," Mael said, ever the regal diplomat.

Michael nodded and turned to Selena. He slid his fingers through her hair and tilted her head up to face him. "I will be with you at all times," he whispered. "And should you want me, all you have to do is call me. *Anee ohev otakh.*"

"I'll be fine, Michael. I don't think I'll need you for anything." Pulling away from him, she turned to look at Mael. Michael nodded, and with nothing more than a shimmer, he faded away. "Where do you want me to stay?"

Glancing between Selena and Cian, Mael felt puzzled by the subtle overtones, but immediately recognized the brittle fragility in Selena's emerald eyes as they meet his gaze. "Jensen will show you to your room, Selena." In answer to a silent summons, the throne room doors opened and Jensen walked in. Without another word spoken, Selena turned on her heel to follow him out. When the door shut behind them, Mael looked at Cian. "Why do I get the feeling I missed something?"

Cian sighed and walked over to Mael's throne, collapsing into it. He shifted to settle his wings over the arms of the throne. "You don't know Hebrew, do you?"

Arching a brow, Mael shook his head. "No. When I was a young man it wasn't required to learn the language of a conquered land."

"I have the ability to detect a good soul and a bad one. Selena's changed, Mael. And..." Cian's words trailed off for a moment. "Michael's fallen in love with her."

"In love? With Selena? That's even more absurd than you and I!"

"Perhaps, but it's the truth." Cian leaned back in the throne, leveling an odd sort of gaze on the prince. "Is it true?"

Mael approached him and bent forward, resting both hands on the arms of Cian's chair. "Is what true?" As he smiled, the touch of his lips brushed Cian's. He caressed the blue feathers of Cian's right wing as his tongue slipped between the angel's lips.

Cian gasped and his body arched off of the throne. He shook his head, even while pulling Mael closer to deepen their kiss. He whimpered softly, trying to shift his wing away from Mael's touch, but Mael wasn't about to let any part of Cian escape him. He followed the evasive attempt, keeping the contact as the kiss became more devouring. He knew they shouldn't be doing this in the throne room, but he didn't particularly care.

Cian's heart thundered and he gripped Mael's other arm tightly. When he had no room left to move in the throne, he gave in. "Do you have any fucking idea what you're doing to me, prince?"

"Arousing you beyond thought and control?" The play of Mael's fingers smoothed through the soft feathers before he moved back out of Cian's reach. Then he turned away and headed for the door. A glance over his shoulder told Cian that Mael expected to be followed.

Cian growled before standing to follow. Mael took his own sweet time going down the hall, his steps slow as he ascended the stairs. "If you're trying to get yourself thrown against the wall, you're doing a damn good job of it."

Cian grabbed Mael's arm tightly and moved swiftly to his bedroom. As soon as the door was closed behind them, Cian shoved Mael up against it and descended on his mouth in a ravenous kiss. Mael's lips parted for Cian, letting his angel's mood descend over him. It left him in that vulnerable state where all he could feel was the need between them. His body arched tightly to Cian as he snaked his arms around Cian's neck.

Cian grabbed Mael's arms, pulling them down. He gripped Mael's wrists tightly and pinned them above Mael's head against the door. The hungry kisses moved from Mael's mouth, over his jaw, and down to his neck. With a single flick of the tongue, Cian made it clear what he wanted first. The ache in his body to feel Cian pulled a low groan from Mael. A wound instantly opened for Cian to feed from, and Mael didn't struggle against the hands that held him pinned.

Cian latched onto the cut, drinking deeply. He gripped both of Mael's wrists in one hand and moved the other down Mael's body. With a quick flick of his hand, Cian had Mael's pants open and they dropped to the floor. Cian wrapped his hand around Mael's cock and squeezed, sending a bolt of white-hot pleasure through Mael's entire body.

"And what does my dark prince want from me this evening?"

The sudden flood of sensation rocked Mael, and he thrust against the hand squeezing around him. "I need you to fuck me. Fuck me until there's nothing but you inside my soul."

Cian pulled away from Mael's throat and slid his tongue over Mael's lips. He released Mael's wrists, and the smile widened as a touch of magic held Mael in place. Cian began removing his own clothing slowly, his dark gaze never leaving Mael's.

"Fuck you?" Cian asked quietly. His hands drifted over his chest and down, drawing Mael's gaze. Wrapping his hands around his own cock, he stroked it slowly from base to tip once before releasing it. He moved closer to Mael, pressing their bodies together as their cocks slid alongside each other. "Or possess you?"

It was more than that and Mael knew it. The contact between them had him straining to get to Cian. "I need you. I need your love, to know nothing but you."

Cian stepped back, reaching out to pull Mael free from the bonds that held him. He jerked Mael roughly up against him. "You are mine, prince." He turned and pushed Mael onto his back on the bed. Getting the lube from the nightstand, Cian wasted no time in slicking himself up. Then he crawled between Mael's legs and rubbed the head of his cock over Mael's entrance. "Make no mistake, Mael," he whispered as he pushed forward the slightest fraction of an inch. "Everything within you belongs to me." Mael's gaze never wavered as Cian thrust forward, impaling him on Cian's cock in one hard, swift motion. "And everything within me belongs to you."

The hard thrust drew a sharp cry from Mael as his mind opened fully to his lover's, letting Cian into him. A strong force wrapped itself around the angel's mind and drew him inside. Mael raked his nails down Cian's back, arching with every hard stroke. "Cian!"

Cian's wings shielded their bodies, and every stroke echoed the words drifting through Mael's mind: You are my love. You are my life. You are my soul. Cian's lips brushed over Mael's, and their tongues met, Cian's presence flooding Mael—inside and out.

Mael fell silent as he began to drown in the emotional onslaught. His body arched from the bed, straining to the pace of Cian's strokes. Each word pierced through his mind, and as he sank beneath everything, he shuddered as he came. He felt beyond lost within the haven of Cian's soul and the love that surrounded him, holding him so tightly.

Cian buried himself one more time inside Mael and groaned, heat rushing through Mael's body.

When they both stopped shaking, Cian rolled Mael over, cradling them both tightly in his wings. "I love you so much," he whispered.

The ties that bound them had buried deeper within him, and Mael had no words for it. The rest of the world had ceased to exist for the time being, leaving only his angel. His body limp against Cian, Mael finally opened his eyes. "Everything is you. Every thought, every dream."

Cian smiled softly and held Mael's gaze as he slid his thumb over Mael's lips. "I've waited so long to hear that," he said quietly. "I wanted so much to be a part of you, as you have always been within me. My love for you goes well beyond anything I have ever known, and to have you in my life is Heaven to me. I love you, Mael. With everything that I am, everything I ever have been, and everything I ever will be."

Pressing a soft kiss to Cian's thumb, Mael drank in the declarations, beyond stunned at the peace he felt for the first time in his existence. "You are my lover, my companion, and my soul. Without you, I'm lost." He couldn't hide this any more. He'd chosen Cian as his companion and he owed it to Cian—to them both—to make that clear.

"You will never be without me." Cian pulled Mael closer to him. "I will always be by your side, whenever you wish me to be."

Mael's lips clung in a lingering touch to Cian's as he whispered, "We are completely bound now. No force can destroy that. And I can no longer keep this secret, Cian. It is no honor to you to do so."

"Then do not keep it. I love you and I will not hesitate to tell anyone that."

"Then I will make the public announcement tomorrow night. I would do it tonight, but it's too damn hard to move."

"That's fine by me, as I have no inclination to let you go right now." Cian licked Mael's right fang before sliding his tongue into Mael's mouth.

The drops of blood that coated his tongue kept Mael silent. He might have an eternity with his angel, but he wasn't about to let the man go anytime soon.

Chapter Three

Brandon rested his chin on his palm, the index finger of his other hand running under each line of text as he translated the information from Latin to English. Having not quite grown used to the warmth of the workroom, he had pulled his shirt off and it was now draped over Cornelius' stool. Cornelius paused and couldn't help the smile that tugged at his mouth. The sight of Brandon pouring over the book reminded Cornelius of himself. Silently, he moved up behind Brandon to peer over one shoulder.

"Good evening," Brandon said quietly. "I thought I'd get some studying in while things were relatively peaceful around here."

"An excellent idea as you never know when all hell will break loose here." Chuckling, Cornelius stepped off to the side and reached across the table for his latest list of projects.

"That seems to be a regular thing around here," Brandon remarked.

"Too damn regular if you ask me." Grabbing one of the pens, Cornelius jotted down several quick notes to restock his inventory.

Brandon pretended to be focused on the book, but Cornelius could feel Brandon watching him. Brandon finally closed his book and turned around on his stool, placing his elbow on the table and cradling his chin in his palm. He studied the list as Cornelius wrote it out. His thoughts reached Cornelius, causing a muscle to twitch at the corner of

Cornelius' mouth. Without moving his head, he looked in Brandon's direction out of the corner of his eye.

"Just making an inventory of items we've run out of. You wanna check the Mars root to see how many are left?"

"Sure." Brandon stood and reached up to the shelf above Cornelius' head to look into a jar. "Three."

With that long, lean body stretched out before him, Cornelius was too acutely aware of the bare chest and the glint of the nipple ring not that far away from his face. Clearing his throat abruptly, he focused back on the paper, marking the root down. "I should get at least ten more. I go through the damn things too fast. You up to helping me go through the inventory? I keep putting it off and now it has to be done." He tried his best to keep his thoughts off of the young vampire, but with Brandon so close, it wasn't easy.

"I'm always up to doing anything you want," Brandon said. "Just tell me what to do." He leaned over to look at the list.

Cornelius slid one of the sheets over. "Check through everything on this list and see how much of each we have. The number listed in front of the name is how much I usually have. If it looks low, just write the name on that pad." By no more than a flicker of a lash did he show any reaction to the double meaning of Brandon's words, and he reined in any wayward thoughts before they could take root in his brain.

Brandon nodded and stood up. He began to move around, checking stock and jotting down names on the paper as he went. "Looks like we're running out of a lot. It's been a while since an inventory was done."

"Too long. I generally hate doing this job. Though it doesn't seem so bad, having somebody with me." As Brandon worked, so did he. Some of the bottles Cornelius could tell just by a quick glance whether he was low or not. After a quick run-through of one of the sheets, he set it down.

Brandon shrugged as he handed his completed list to Cornelius. "I don't mind doing it. Although I have to agree, it's nice to have company. What's next?"

Cornelius snickered as he opened a folder. Drawing out at least twenty more sheets, he laid them on the table. "Do you care to guess?"

Brandon laughed and picked up the entire stack. "Here, I'll take this off your hands." He stilled for a moment and then slipped a hand under Cornelius' chin. Turning Cornelius' head, Brandon pressed a soft, chaste kiss to his lips. "I don't mind doing inventory."

The urge to respond to that kiss crossed Cornelius' mind, but he ignored it, or at least tried to. The slow slide of his gaze took in the shirtless upper half of the young vampire's body, and no matter how much he knew he shouldn't, he couldn't help but think about tasting the bared flesh for himself. As Brandon wrote down yet another ingredient on the list, Cornelius became all too aware of the young vampire's thoughts. Images flitted through Brandon's mind: Cornelius leaning up against the workroom wall, gripping his head, and thrusting into his waiting mouth. Cornelius' eyes narrowed on Brandon, then schooled to something less knowing when Brandon turned around once more. The expression on Brandon's face and the dart of his tongue made Cornelius' body tighten slightly in response. Hurriedly, Cornelius looked down at the list, one hand settling in his lap as he began to write.

Brandon set another completed list before Cornelius. "You know," he whispered as he leaned down close to Cornelius' ear. "I'd be more than happy to solve that problem."

Cornelius groaned quietly to himself. That was exactly what he wanted; he just couldn't act on it. Mael Black had strictly forbade anything intimate between them, thanks in most part to Cornelius' less-than-perfect track record, including the prince himself. Forcing the wayward stream of thought to settle back on the printed words, he murmured, "You're doing enough work already."

Brandon chuckled softly. "I'd much rather be on my knees with your cock in my mouth," he said without looking up from the paper he was filling out.

Cornelius shot him a quick look. "I know what you want, Brandon."

"Mm," Brandon murmured. "And what do you want?" He didn't look at Cornelius, but instead continued to work, now standing in front of the table with his back to Cornelius. He bent over to check the jars lining another table, leaning on one elbow while he checked amounts and wrote ingredients on the list.

"Something I can't have, and you know that." A tinge of regret threaded through Cornelius' words. Finally, he gave up on his list in favor of watching Brandon. His gaze slowly slid over the line of Brandon's ass, and he ended up having to restrain the urge to touch.

Brandon sighed and dropped his pen. He cradled his head in his hands and muttered, "But I'm not going to give up. I want you so fucking bad, it's driving me insane."

Cornelius got up and rested his hand on Brandon's shoulder. He only meant the touch to soothe over the agitation he felt from the young vampire. Before he realized it, he was leaning closer, brushing a kiss to the side of Brandon's throat. Nor was he quite sure how he ended up molding his body to Brandon's backside.

Brandon's breath caught and he reached back with one hand, tilting his head to bare his neck in clear invitation. He rocked his hips back, grinding slowly against Cornelius. "Cornelius," he pleaded in a whisper. "Please..."

Slipping both arms around Brandon's waist to keep Brandon tightly against him, Cornelius groaned softly against Brandon's skin. A soft series of kisses scattered over Brandon's neck as Cornelius drew a deep breath, savoring the scent of Brandon's blood. His fangs sank into the tender flesh, his defenses rapidly shutting down as the taste hit him. Despite being the young vampire's Father, Cornelius' need went far deeper than was welcome. His cock hardened with the press of Brandon's body, unable to avoid reacting to it. He drank deeply, trying to drown himself in the rich crimson flow pouring down his throat.

Brandon whimpered softly as his grip on Cornelius' head tightened. "I need you. Oh, God, Cornelius, I need you so bad." Brandon's other hand dropped to Cornelius' waist and he threaded his fingers through Cornelius'.

Cornelius had to stop before he took too much. A soft lick healed the marks he had made in Brandon's skin. Not being able to pull back right away, he scattered several more kisses across Brandon's neck. "I know, Brandon. I need you, too." Closing his eyes, Cornelius released Brandon and then stepped back. With a great deal of regret, he realized things were probably becoming too hard on Brandon.

"Too hard?" Brandon said with a muffled laugh. He straightened up and turned. He jumped up on the table and locked both legs around Cornelius' waist, pulling Cornelius close. He trailed a single fingertip down Cornelius' chest and looked up to meet that gaze. "All I have to do to solve the immediate problem is the same thing I've been doing: jerk off while thinking of you. But God, I'd give anything in this world to feel you inside me instead."

"You've been reading me, haven't you?" Cornelius couldn't find it in himself to be angry, but the potential for others finding trouble with it was there. "Be careful of who you do that to, Brandon. Others can take serious exception to it at times."

"I was told it could be done, but that I must be careful. Don't worry, gorgeous. You're the only one I have any desire to read." Brandon threaded his fingers through Cornelius' hair, cupping Cornelius' face gently. "One kiss," he whispered. "If I can't have you, at least give me that."

Cornelius lifted his hand, catching Brandon's. "And will you be satisfied with that, Child?" He lowered his head, the barest touch of his lips covering Brandon's before drawing slowly back.

Brandon grimaced at the swift brush of a kiss. Before Cornelius could move any farther, Brandon drew Cornelius' head back to him and slid his tongue over Cornelius' lips, practically begging for them to part. Cornelius flicked his tongue over the tip of Brandon's before slipping deeper into Brandon's mouth. Brandon moaned and pulled Cornelius closer with his legs. He slid his arms around Cornelius' shoulders, holding tight, as if he were afraid to let go. Cornelius took his time with the leisurely exploration. He caressed Brandon's tongue with his own in slow circles. He really didn't want to let go either.

Brandon pulled slowly away from their kiss and rested his head on Cornelius' shoulder. "Please don't let me go," he whispered. "I promise I'll keep my hands to myself and not bother you, but I don't want to sleep alone. Every night I dream of falling asleep in your arms, Cornelius. Please let me experience it... just once."

"I want you to stay with me, just to let me hold you through the day, and to know you were with me."

"I'm always with you," Brandon said quietly. "Even when I'm not physically near you, I am always with you. All I ask is one day, to know what it's like to fall asleep in your arms and to see your face when I wake."

"We both need each other in more ways than I think are healthy, Brandon. My mind is always on you, watching out for you so that I know when the least little thing is wrong. And sometimes that can be a bit of a trial when your thoughts tend to roam."

Brandon smiled. "Would you feel better if I were to take care of things in my room before going to yours?"

A surprised laugh burst from Cornelius. "You know, I don't know what to say to that."

Brandon lifted an eyebrow and then his lips curled into a wickedly playful grin. "You can't do anything with me," he said. "But that doesn't mean you can't watch me do anything to myself." One of his hands dropped to his own lap to rub over the bulge in his jeans.

"If I say yes, it's just torturing me," Cornelius muttered, his gaze lowering to watch.

"Then what's stopping you from doing the same? I promise," Brandon said breathlessly as he continued to rub the hard ridge of his denim-covered cock. "I won't touch you."

"And what's to stop me from touching you?" Cornelius placed his hand over Brandon's, just to still the motion and give himself time to think.

Brandon gasped and, turning his hand, he quickly threaded his fingers through Cornelius'. He began to move their hands together, increasing the pressure. His head tilted back and his eyes closed slowly. "Don't stop," he whispered. "Please, Cornelius, don't stop."

Cornelius brushed aside Brandon's hand and replaced it with his own, letting his fingers rub the contours of Brandon's cock through the material. With his other hand, he unfastened Brandon's pants. As soon as they were open, he slipped his hand beneath the material.

"Cornelius..." Brandon leaned back against the wall, his legs tightening around Cornelius as he thrust his hips up. "Oh God, please..." he begged. "Don't stop..."

As Cornelius' fingers curled around Brandon underneath the material, they stroked slowly over him. An intense focus zeroed in on Brandon, his pleas music to Cornelius' ears. "I'm not going to stop until you come for me." Brandon's eyes flew open and he locked onto Cornelius' emerald gaze, and Cornelius grasped Brandon's chin tightly, holding his face in place to watch him intently as he came.

"Oh, God..." Seconds later, Brandon cried out the mage's name as he jerked, slick heat coating Cornelius' hand.

"You cry out so beautifully to me," Cornelius purred softly. He leaned forward, capturing Brandon's mouth in a deep, heated kiss.

Brandon's arms circled Cornelius' neck, holding tightly as he deepened their kiss. Despite having finally come, Cornelius could feel the turmoil of Brandon's thoughts. Cornelius knew how Brandon felt, but to follow that path would bring them both nothing but trouble. It pained Cornelius to know that he couldn't have what he truly wanted. Finally drawing back from Brandon's lips, Cornelius tugged his hand from the confines of Brandon's jeans and licked the young vampire's seed from his hand. He pinned Brandon with his own look of hunger and need. Brandon caught Cornelius' hand then and drew it to his lips. He sucked two of Cornelius' fingers into his mouth. Cornelius bent down to take a brief taste in a quick kiss before speaking.

"Just for the night, Child."

"If you won't make love to me," Brandon said quietly, "then at least let me watch you come. Let me lick it off of your fingers. Let me taste you."

"Why don't we retire before the sun comes up?"

Brandon jumped off of the table, landing on not-so-steady legs. He caught Cornelius' shoulder with his hand and waved the other toward the door. "After you."

Once Brandon was steady, Cornelius led the way to his bedroom. "Did you want to change your clothes before you join me?"

"I sleep with nothing on. Would you rather I wear something?"

"A pair of your silk pants will do, young man." Stifling his laughter, Cornelius turned to head into his bedroom.

"Be right there."

When Brandon walked into his room, Cornelius went into to his own. He changed into a worn pair of gray sweat pants and no shirt. Once on the bed, Cornelius let one of his hands stray over his chest, thoughts of Brandon running through his head. Brandon returned and crawled onto the other side of the bed, never taking his eyes off of Cornelius. Settling near Cornelius and watching the movement of his hand like a hawk, Brandon groaned, lounge pants tenting. Cornelius reached out and drew Brandon close, letting his fingers pinch and twist at one of Brandon's nipples.

"I think you have a problem again," he said in an amused tone.

Brandon gasped and arched his body. "Yes," he whispered breathlessly. He slid his arm around Cornelius' waist, drawing their bodies closer together.

"But as I recall, I'm supposed to be taking care of my problem," Cornelius teased. Tomorrow he might regret anything that happened, but tonight he wanted for them.

Brandon nodded, licking his lips. "Believe me. Watching you, it won't take long to solve my own."

Cornelius edged his hand beneath the waistband of his pants and stroked slowly over his own cock. He couldn't begin to stop the soft moan, wishing like hell it was Brandon's body over him, a tight ass squeezing every inch of his hard flesh. The unexpected touch of Brandon's tongue to his left nipple sent a shiver rushing through Cornelius' body. He quickly got rid of his pants, then resumed stroking, softly murmuring Brandon's name as the young vampire's tongue circled his nipple.

Brandon moved his mouth lower and began kissing a trail up Cornelius' chest. He brushed his lips over Cornelius' throat and then whispered in his ear, "Come for me, cariad."

Brandon's words were like an aphrodisiac. Cornelius groaned, pumping his cock faster. Within seconds, a hot mouth enveloped Cornelius, swallowing his entire length. His eyes flew open as he lifted his head to look down at the sight of Brandon between his legs, head bobbing, lips slick as his cock pushed between them.

"Come for me, Cornelius..." Brandon slid his other palm over Cornelius' balls, kneading them gently as he slid his mouth up and down Cornelius' shaft. His tongue grazed the sensitive underside with every slide of his lips.

The intimate whisper to his thoughts sank into Cornelius' mind. A quick thrust of his hips buried his cock deep as his body shuddered in release, coming in Brandon's mouth. A guttural groan rumbled from him, twisting into the young vampire's name.

Brandon swallowed quickly and seconds later he jerked and moaned, heat splashing Cornelius' leg. Panting, Brandon licked Cornelius clean before collapsing beside him. Cornelius lay back, spent, and he looked over at Brandon's hand with a chuckle. He drew Brandon's hand to his mouth and licked the palm. Brandon moaned softly and pulled his hand away, only to replace it with his mouth. He licked Cornelius' lips slowly.

"I know this probably isn't something you really want to hear," he said. Then he stopped, as if thinking better of what he wanted to say.

"I had simply wanted us to be together, Brandon. Just for the day in each other's arms." Things got out of hand between them, and Cornelius knew that, but he still couldn't regret having Brandon beside him.

Brandon nodded. "I know, and I'm sorry."

"It's my fault, not yours, Child." Cornelius eyed Brandon quietly before he spoke again, the tenor of Brandon's jumbled thoughts reaching him even through the post-orgasmic haze. "What is it?" He took hold of Brandon's chin to draw that gaze back to him.

Brandon remained silent for a brief moment and took a deep breath. "I'm afraid I've fallen in love with you."

The words made Cornelius smile and brought a distinct softening to his expression. "Did you think I didn't already know that, Brandon? Your thoughts and everything that you feel are mine to know."

Brandon blushed. "You knew?" He sat up and drew his legs up, wrapping his arms around them. "I'm sorry if it's not something you really wanted to hear, Cornelius, but I can't help what I feel. When I'm with you, nothing else in this world matters. I feel special and wanted, and I only want you to be happy."

Sitting up, Cornelius slipped his arm around Brandon's shoulders, drawing Brandon in against his side. "If I hadn't wanted it, I would have seriously discouraged you. I do have my ways, you know. You should know I feel the same about you." A deeper touch from his mind engulfed Brandon, letting Brandon feel the emotions he'd held at bay for some time.

Brandon gasped. "You do?"

"Yes. I love you, Brandon. And you make me unbelievably happy."

"I love you, too."

Drawing Brandon back down to lie beside him, Cornelius whispered, "Now sleep, and know that I am beside you."

Chapter Four

When Mael left the library, he headed back up the stairs. Halfway to his bedroom, an earsplitting shriek broke the silence. It came from of one of the bedrooms further down the corridor. Recognizing the voice as Selena's, he ran toward her room. In the open doorway, Mael saw her, standing beside her bed, trembling. A quick scan showed no apparent danger as he hurried over to her.

"Selena, what's wrong?"

Terror etched on her pale features, she pointed a shaking hand in the direction of the bed. A single black rose rested on her pillow. While the sight wasn't all that unusual, her whisper was. "Memnet."

Mael's gaze narrowed on the rose as he held Selena close, drawing her in against him in an effort to comfort her. Silently, he summoned Ben and carefully held her while he waited for his secretary. "I'll get it taken care of." When Ben came into the room, he bowed toward Mael and then stilled, awaiting his instructions. "Get rid of that rose on the bed and meet me in my office. I'll be there as soon as I can."

Ben picked up the rose and left the room as quietly as he'd arrived. Selena had finally stopped trembling and seemed calmer as Mael drew back his head to look at her. Seeing the fear she tried to hide, he shook his head. "Selena, you're safe here. Memnet can't get into the palace. His tricks are nothing more than that; he can't get to you."

"I know. It was just a shock to see his calling card."

"A pathetic little trick at best, Selena, designed to frightened a Child. Are you all right now?" When she nodded, he let go of her, stepping back with a smile. "Then you can do me a favor. I need you to find Cornelius and work with him on figuring out what we can use against Memnet. You know him better than any of us."

An unpleasant smile curved her lips as she said, "That will give me great pleasure."

Jensen caught Mael in the hallway. "Your Excellency, this just arrived from Rome." After handing Mael an envelope, Jensen stepped back with a bow.

"Thank you." Descending the stairs, Mael opened the envelope and read over the note, then shook his head. The note was from one of Diocourides' secretaries, warning him of his Father's intentions within the Romanorum. As he entered his office, he tossed the note on his desk before addressing his secretary.

"Ben, I want the palace protections double-checked and secured. Any guards we have the slightest questions about, are to be replaced and put on internal duty. Memnet found a way to get that rose in here, and I want to know how." Mael settled in his chair and motioned for Ben to sit in the one opposite.

"There would be no way Memnet could get in. Not without alerting you, Mael."

"Either he managed to get somebody in here, or one of my employees is working with him. Either way, I want an answer."

"I'll get the roster of who was on duty at the gates and doing the perimeter sweeps, as well as who entered the palace over the last few hours. Do you want Jake to conduct the interrogations?"

"Have Jake and Eric take care of that. I want two people working on everything that's done. I also want you to get the memory orb from Cornelius." The stone would make recordings of the proceedings that he could review later.

"Consider it done." Ben stood and walked out, leaving Mael to his thoughts.

The thought that someone in his court might be working with Memnet was unsettling at best. Mael sat back with a sigh, wondering who could possibly be behind it. After a moment, the phone rang. Mael wanted to ignore it, but knew that was futile. He picked it up after the third ring.

"Yes?"

"You have a visitor, Your Excellency," Jensen said. "I've sent him to your office."

"Who—?" Before Mael could finish, the door opened. Glancing up, he was surprised to see his Son walking into his office. He smiled. "What brings you here, Christian?"

Stilling in front of the desk, Christian bowed his head. "I thought it was past time for a visit, Father. If you have the time to spare for us to talk?"

"Of course I have the time for you." Mael stood and led Christian to his private sitting room. "The last I heard from you, you were in Rome."

"I had been planning on spending the rest of the year there, but my plans changed somewhat." Giving Mael a rueful smile, Christian didn't give his full reasoning, which gave Mael a fair idea of why he was here.

Mael fell silent as they walked upstairs and down the hall. Once the door closed behind them, he settled in one of the wing chairs, gesturing his Son to sit in the chair nearest to him. "Now what's going on, Christian?"

Settling into the seat, Christian rolled his eyes, sighing. "Nigel sent me. He wants you to rescind your proclamation for companion. I had planned on staying in Rome, but his temperament makes London a better harbor for now."

"I do believe my Father is out of his ever-loving mind."

Christian gave him an easy-going, affectionate smile, dropping the formalities now that they were alone. "I've thought that many times over the years, Mael. I decided to play least in sight in Rome and head here to deliver his message. After that, you're on your own. Grandfather has been haunting the marble halls of the Romanorum ever since you made the claim. He was able to garner some support since not everybody likes this idea of you and a vampire hunter, but it wasn't enough to overturn Diocourides' edict. Nigel's been raging since."

Mael's tone was dry. "I'm not all that surprised. I can imagine his face when he found out I was involved with a vampire hunter and wanted him proclaimed as my companion."

"He believes you are shaming the family name. Quite frankly, I've heard enough, not to mention the stories that a sorcerer has enslaved you using magic." Eyeing Mael, Christian smirked faintly. "I hope you don't mind that I decided to come here. I figured you could use a visit from me."

"No, I don't mind at all." Mael studied his Son, seeing far more than just what was on the surface. He remained silent about it, though, giving Christian time to decide his own mind, though some of what he saw pained him.

"I take it my usual room is still to be had."

"Of course, and you're more than welcome to stay as long as you want."

Christian stood and leaned over to hug Mael tightly, whispering, "You're always here when I need you."

"And I always will be, Child."

When Christian left, Cian stepped inside, closing the door behind him. "Who was that?" he asked as he sat down near Mael.

"My eldest, Christian." Mael had realized his own Father wouldn't approve of his relationship with Cian, but he hadn't thought rumors and whispers of sorcery being used on him would be a part of it.

"A Son?" Cian mused quietly. "Why didn't you tell me about him?"

"Because Christian hasn't visited me in quite some time, and I didn't think he would all of a sudden descend on me." Sighing quietly, Mael relaxed back into the cushions. "Which means you and I should talk, my angel."

"Yes," Cian said quietly. "I do believe we need to. Why has he come if you haven't seen each other in so long?"

"Christian brought me a message from my Father. Nigel wants me to call off my relationship with you." An almost unholy smirk settled on Mael's lips as if to say 'like that will ever fucking happen'.

A blond eyebrow lifted quizzically. "Well now, that's an interesting message. Why? Does your Father disapprove of you being with a hunter? Or is it the sorcery?"

"Both, it seems. The tales of you enslaving me are all over the place." Chuckling softly, Mael eyed Cian with a smile. "My

Father believes I am shaming the family name. He also forgets he hasn't dictated my life in many years."

"Although the thought of enslaving you is an amusing one, it is far from the truth. Why would they think that?"

"You are a hunter, and only a few in Rome are aware of your help in taking care of the rogues. I really must inform the others soon just how much of a help you were. My Father will believe whatever he wants to believe. He is even more stubborn than I am."

Cian repressed a grin, but the sparkle in his eyes clearly said that he didn't believe anyone could be that stubborn. "No one has ever witnessed my magic," he said. "And only those who practice magic themselves would see me for what I am." His gaze narrowed. "What of Christian? He didn't seem to be particularly fond of me when I saw him in the hallway."

Another quiet sigh escaped, one of deeper contemplation. "My eldest and I haven't shared a home in several centuries, so I'm no longer sure of his moods, Cian."

"Something about him sets me on edge, Mael. I cannot lie to you about that." Cian looked down and traced a finger over the fabric of the arm of the chair. "What happened between you two that put you at odds with each other?"

Mael considered Cian's question for a moment before he quietly answered. "He hated how possessive I got over him. It marred our relationship to the point where I had to let him go or risk his resentment. We haven't resided in the same house since then. He has occasionally visited me, and there were times he returned to me, but only for short periods."

"Funny how one man can find your possessiveness a trial, while another desperately clings to it," Cian said without looking up. "And what of your Father?"

"Yes, funny how that is. As for my Father, he has been and always will be a pain in the ass that I generally ignore. Christian will be staying with us until things blow over. I'm not sure if he plans on returning to Rome or not."

"Very well," Cian said quietly, although the look in his eyes when he lifted his head held a much different opinion. "Why would your Father choose to interfere with your life if you are no longer with him?"

"Nigel ruled Rome when he created me and he still rules as Prince of Rome. He's always been used to being obeyed. For the most part, we've always been in agreement except for a few matters." Mael reached out to cover Cian's hand with his own, craving the contact.

Cian turned his hand over to lace his fingers through Mael's. "What do the others of the Romanorum think about our relationship?"

"Many disagree with it, but not enough to sway Diocourides from his decision to accept it. And it really wouldn't matter to me even if none accepted it. I've chosen you, Cian, and I stand by that choice." Lifting his hand, Mael brushed a soft kiss to the back of Cian's hand.

Cian smiled. "If so many disagree, what convinced Diocourides?"

"You would have to meet him to understand. He is a much different man than most of us. I talked with him a few times and I believe you would like him."

"Sounds like Lee," Cian mused.

"Your brother?"

"Aye," Cian said with a nod. "Lee is an unusual man, Mael. I think, had Rachel not been an issue, that given time, he would've warmed up to you. And he may still. Lee holds grudges, but not for long." He stared down at the floor and laughed. "Although I'm lucky I got the glass picked out of my feathers. That was a might painful."

Mael's fingers tightened gently around his hand, understanding it was an issue that still troubled Cian. "If there had been any way around it, I wouldn't have killed Rachel. I wouldn't blame him for holding a grudge for a very long time over me killing his girlfriend."

"I know. Lee has a lot to think on now. He has the damnable habit of not listening to his older brother, even though I am always proven correct in the end. But I do miss him."

"Is he still in London?" At the time, there had been little Mael could do but kill Rachel Centers. She had been too deeply involved in all of the rogue vampire problems. He'd seriously doubted if her assassination attempt on him and Cian would have been her last.

"No, he went on to Cardiff. He has friends there. Brandon was happy to write him for me, as Lee's friends do not know Welsh. It's the only way that I could ensure the letter would not be read by others."

"Why would you have Brandon write you a letter? I know you speak Welsh," Mael asked him, rather confused.

Cian laughed. "I know Welsh, but I never learned to write."

Mael eyed Cian for a moment in silence, more than a touch surprised by that. "Why haven't you ever learned to write?"

Cian shrugged. "Never had a need. I was trained with a sword, as a fighter. While I learned to read and understand several mortal languages, I never saw a need to write."

"Do you feel the need to learn yet?"

"I'm beginning to. I suppose I probably need to now. Why? Are you offering to teach me?" Cian laughed.

"I would be more than happy to teach you, Cian. I've always enjoyed playing a stern school master." How Mael managed to keep a straight face was beyond Cian, but he did.

Cian gave him a wry grin and waved toward the door leading out to Mael's main office. "Yes, I'm sure you do, Your Excellency." The grin widened considerably as he added, "Or would that be Master?"

"I think I prefer the sound of Master, personally. I'll just have to remember where I put that wooden paddle for when your attention is distracted."

"As you wish...Master. I shall do my best to not keep my attention on my lessons."

Mael stood, giving Cian a stern look. The twinkle in his eyes made his enjoyment clear. He was looking forward to giving his angel lessons and for the next few hours, he did just that.

* * *

The next night went relatively smoothly. Christian pretty much kept to himself, save for a few people he knew from before. It left Mael to get some much-needed work done. After finishing the paperwork in his office, Mael decided to check on Cian. He'd given his angel some exercises to work on and given that he hadn't seen Cian in a while, Mael knew his angel was probably in the library working. Mael headed down the hall and paused in the doorway of the library.

It took a few moments before Cian stopped writing to look up. "Looking for something, love?"

Mael walked up behind Cian and rested his hands on Cian's shoulders. Leaning over, he brushed a kiss to the top of Cian's head. "I think I found what I was looking for."

Cian chuckled and tilted his head back, reaching up to curl his fingers around Mael's. "Lee's in town."

"Have you seen him?"

Cian laughed. "I'll say I did."

"Something amusing about seeing your brother?"

"A touch. I managed to find him in town, locked in a rather passionate kiss with an unexpected person."

Mael released Cian and sat on the edge of the desk beside him. "So who was your brother kissing and why is it so funny?"

Cian didn't bother to hide the grin. "When was the last time you saw your assassin?"

Mael's brow creased slightly as he frowned, realizing he hadn't seen Sav lately. "It's been a few nights." The frown eased as he realized what Cian was getting at. "You mean your brother and my assassin? You saw them?"

"I did. I couldn't believe what I was seeing, but there was Lee, one arm around Sav's waist, the two of them locked in a kiss."

Well, that certainly explained where Sav had been hiding. "I thought your brother despised vampires. I know Sav isn't fond of any kind of creature, though in her job, it is a necessary evil to remain distanced."

Cian raised his arms and locked his fingers behind his head. "Aye," he said with a nod. "Lee has never liked vampires, which is why I was so shocked. But then I know my brother. I might have a taste for men, but Sav is a good-looking woman. It doesn't surprise me that Lee would be attracted to her, especially considering that they both share aspects of their personalities."

"I've had her watching him on and off," Mael admitted. "Just to make sure everything is okay. I never expected she would even talk to him, let alone do anything more."

Cian lifted an eyebrow at him. "You've had her trailing him? Apparently things have progressed a bit from that."

Though he was surprised at the notion, it didn't disturb Mael. What his assassin did on her own free time was her business. "Yes, I asked her to. Ever since I disposed of Rachel, I wanted to keep an eye on things in Lee's direction to make sure he was all right. He doesn't know who she is, does he?"

"No, he doesn't. The only ones from this court I have ever mentioned have been you and Brandon. He has no idea who she is." Cian's brow furrowed a bit then. "But his wings were visible. He dropped the illusion," he said. "For her."

"She already knows what he is. She's seen you with the wings and knows he's your brother. I really hope she's not getting in over her head, but I'll leave that for her to decide." Reaching out, Mael took a hold of Cian's hand, twining their fingers together. "She's a big girl."

"I know that. But he's my brother, so I'm going to worry a bit."

"Sav won't harm him, Cian, and she's never been one to play with others. The only thing that bothers me is what will happen if he can't fully accept who she is." Most certainly, Mael's assassin was nothing like Lee's ex-girlfriend, Rachel. Sav held herself to a far different honor code, one that Rachel Centers could never have understood.

"Lee is a lot like me, cariad," Cian said after a moment. "When he falls, he falls hard. He will get over it, although I'd venture to guess that he won't be thrilled if someone besides Sav tells him."

"We'll have to leave it to her to tell him then. She's nothing like Rachel, and I think you've noticed she tends to be overprotective at times."

Cian smiled. "That I have noticed. But with you as her prince, I can't say that I blame her." He picked up the pen and absently twirled it between his fingers. "How does she handle a bad temper? That's one way Lee and I greatly differ; his temper is short."

Mael had to laugh because Sav had been handling him fairly well for years. "She has a sense of humor she uses on me quite often. She's generally rather hard to rile."

"That's refreshing," Cian laughed. "Lee doesn't let things roll off his back like I do. He nearly had a heart attack when I told him about our first kiss."

"Considering he's had his first kiss with one of my kind, his opinion has hopefully changed on the matter." Smirking faintly, Mael lifted Cian's hand, brushing a kiss to the back of it before lowering their hands back to his thigh.

Cian held his gaze quietly for a moment before speaking. "Lee is hard to resist, that much I can't deny. I've seen too many women fall over themselves while competing for his attention. I've even seen a few men do the same, although those ventures always proved to be fruitless. But the thing to remember about Lee is that he can melt even the most frigid heart. I think Rachel was a bad choice on his part, but Sav..." He shook his head. "I think Sav may find that, once my brother has had a taste of her, chances are, it won't be the last. We angels are hard to resist."

"Since his brother is impossible to resist, I feel a tinge of sympathy for Sav. She has no clue, I'll wager. And if he's too much like you, she doesn't stand a chance."

Cian stood slowly and moved between Mael's legs. As he slid his hands up Mael's thighs, his eyes slowly darkened. With a soft click, the library door locked. "You know what I want right now?"

As his legs parted, giving Cian room, Mael put his hands on Cian's hips. He knew exactly what was on his angel's mind. "More homework?"

"If you consider bending the Prince of London over the desk and fucking him until he screams work... then yes."

Mael feigned a look of surprise as he murmured, "I must have misread what you wanted, Cian. You know I would certainly never deny you all the hard work you want."

Cian slid an arm around Mael's waist and jerked Mael hard against his body. His other hand slipped through Mael's hair, wrapped tightly in it, and pulled Mael's head back. "I want nothing more than to bury my cock in your ass, prince. Here and now."

The teasing edge faded quickly from Mael as he felt the harder press of Cian's body against his. As his head tipped back, he growled softly. "Then what are you waiting for?"

Just as Cian leaned down to kiss him, there was a knock on the door. Cian sighed and rested his forehead against Mael's. "Yes?"

"Master Cian, your brother is on the phone," Ben said from the other side of the locked door.

"Shall we continue this when things are less hectic?" Mael asked.

"I suppose so," Cian muttered. He kissed Mael, then stepped back, dropping down into his chair again. He picked up the phone. "Lee, hi." The more he listened, the more he frowned. "All right. I'll be there shortly." When he hung up, Cian stared at the phone. Mael waited patiently. "Lee needs me."

"Then go. I've got some things I need to tend to." Mael stood and bent to kiss Cian. "I'll see you when you get back."

Cian nodded, the worried look remaining. "Okay."

Chapter Five

Perched on the ledge of a rooftop, Sav crouched, observing the streets and alley below. She liked this vantage point. It allowed her to see a great deal, while still giving her the advantage of getting just about anywhere swiftly. The streets were darker than usual and the last of the club crowd was beginning to thin out. Before long, there were only a few stragglers left on the street at all.

"Hey, you need help, man?" a straggler from the club crowd asked as he stopped at the mouth of an alley. Seconds later, a body dropped at the man's feet, covered in blood. It seemed as if someone had literally ripped the victim's heart straight out of his chest. "What the fuck!" The man started backing away as a figure stepped into a small patch of light cast by a nearby street lamp. Before the man could react, a hand shot out, gripping his throat tightly and dragging him into the alleyway.

Sav leaped the small distance to the next roof to get closer before she jumped to the street below. Landing behind the attacker, she swiftly straightened and moved forward.

With a quick jerk of a hand, the man's neck snapped. His attacker threw him to the ground and turned around slowly. "Another one come to play? My, this has been an eventful evening."

The speed with which the attacker killed the poor man told Sav this wasn't an ordinary human.

Focusing on him, she caught a sharp, malevolent taint from his aura that she wasn't familiar with. She darted to his right, putting her in the perfect position to aim a forceful kick to the man's head before she had to jump to the side when the flimsy metal she'd been holding gave way.

The man stumbled, then righted himself, relatively unaffected by the attack. A slow grin spread across his face before his hand shot out toward Sav, catching her by the throat. He jerked her to him.

"Vampire or no, I'll enjoy killing you. And when the last of your life is seeping away, remember my name: Zalael."

The skin on her forearms split open, and Sav dug her fingers into her own flesh and drew out two small daggers. With long-practiced motions, the two knives quickly embedded into each side of his neck. She knew that name and she knew what she was dealing with, but she didn't have the skill to handle him alone. She brought up the heel of her hand and smashed it into his wrist, hoping the triple pain would break the hold.

Zalael roared and the sharp pain forced him to relinquish his hold on her. He jerked out the knives and the wounds healed as he caught her shoulder. What were once fingers became razor sharp claws as he sliced at her back, ripping both cloth and flesh apart. He pulled her backward and impaled her on one clawed hand. He twisted it around, ripping and tearing through her body. When another figure dropped down in front of her with two massive wings spread out and ready to attack, Zalael released Sav and shoved her to the side.

The agonizing pain shot through her, and Sav screamed. She slammed against the wall of the building and slowly slid down to the filthy ground, barely aware of her savior. She hadn't taken damage like this in a long time, but her senses were too alert to leave herself unguarded. Quickly diverting the energy of her blood from healing, she focused on getting to her feet. Clinging to the side of the building, she made it up, though she staggered with the pain.

The winged figure stepped out of the darkness and into a patch of light. It reflected off of the blue feathers of his wings and the gold in his hair. From behind her, an arm slipped quickly around Sav's waist to keep her from falling or reentering the fight. Two. She had two saviors, both of whom she knew. But there was still the demon, who was preparing to attack Cian. Sav tried to move, instinct telling her to fight. The arm around her tightened.

"Do not think I will let you go," Lee Carmichael whispered in her ear. "No amount of pride will be enough to win this one."

"Well, well," Zalael sneered. "If it isn't the mighty angel."

Without saying a word, Cian rushed Zalael, shoving him hard against the wall. Zalael shook his head and stood, brushing off dirt and debris. Sav's head was hazy with the pain radiating from her back. She gave up trying to fight Lee, trusting in him when her strength began to fail.

Cian caught the demon just as Zalael rushed him, fingers digging into Zalael's neck. Surprise seemed to shock Zalael into place, as if he hadn't expected Cian's strength. With his free hand, the angel opened a black portal. "Go back to your Master," he commanded. Cian turned and lifted Zalael off the ground, throwing him into the portal. Before the demon could reach out, the portal closed. Cian turned to Lee and Sav. "Come." Another portal opened and he stepped through.

"Come on, love," Lee whispered as he bent to pick Sav up. He cradled her in his arms as he walked through the portal behind Cian.

Grumbling as she was picked up, she forced out the words, "I can walk."

"Nonsense," Lee said. "I'm carrying you, whether you like it or not." He tightened his hold on her and stepped into Cian's chambers in the tower. Lee carried her over to the bed and placed her down gently. He sat down beside her and brushed a lock of hair from her face.

She'd already lost a lot of blood and used too much energy trying to reknit the gaping wounds. She heard Cian and Lee speaking, but it seemed so far away and she forced herself to refocus on her surroundings. A hand on her chest gently kept her down when she tried to sit up. It was Lee. She didn't need to hear him—she knew his touch. She wanted to open her eyes, but as the voices drifted away, so did she.

* * *

"Do you love her?"

Lee looked down at Sav. "Yes."

"Then it will be your task to care for her. She will need to feed from you. A lot. Rest yourself; you will need it. Here." Cian pulled a dagger from his belt. "Make a cut on your wrist and press it to her lips. She will begin to feed."

Lee nodded and did as he was told. He lay down beside her as he pressed the cut on his wrist to Sav's mouth. "Please," he whispered.

"If you have any trouble, you know how to find me."

Lee nodded without looking up. As Cian started to step into the portal, Lee called him. Cian turned around. "Thank you, Cian. I know it's not quite enough for my behavior regarding your prince, but it's the best I can do right now. When she's healed, I'll take her to Black's palace myself. I think it's time I met the Prince of London." Cian smiled and nodded, then stepped through the portal before it closed.

Back home, Cian draped his cloak over the footboard of the bed before going into Mael's private study, absently thanking God there was an entrance from their bedroom so he didn't have to risk running into anyone else. He tried desperately to put forth a neutral expression, although he felt nothing neutral inside. Lee's admission wasn't the issue that was troubling Cian, however; meeting an old enemy face-to-face was. He sat down in one of the overstuffed chairs and let his head fall back as he waited until Mael was finished with what he was doing.

"What's wrong?"

"I'm not entirely sure where to start," Cian said quietly. "Sav is safe. Lee has her in my tower until she's healed enough to come home."

"What? What happened?"

"She had an encounter with Zalael. He's here, Mael—in London."

Mael took hold of Cian's hand and drew him up and over. "We need to deal with him, then. Though the 'how' is something we have to discuss."

"Yes, we do," Cian said. "Sav wasn't as badly damaged as you were before, but I had to get them to someplace safe. Zalael cannot get to my tower. As for how to kill him..." He fell silent for a moment before continuing. "Alone, I can handle him now, much to Zalael's surprise, I think. With Memnet behind him, I cannot. We're going to need Michael and Cornelius.

Only magic can destroy Zalael. It's an issue of not turning your back for a single moment."

"Unfortunately, while Memnet is younger than I am, he is a formula higher in power. I can set Cornelius to coming up with something that might help in taking him out. I also have the feeling Michael's help is going to be more than needed."

"We have to keep Brandon out of this. If he finds out that Cornelius is going to be directly involved, he will try to join in," Cian said.

"Since I doubt Cornelius would like him involved at all, that should be no problem."

Cian nodded and rested his cheek to Mael's hair. "I'd be lying if I said I wasn't terrified," he said quietly. "I have a bad feeling about this. One strong enough that it's kept me awake long after sleep has taken you."

"You aren't alone, my angel. This time you have me, though I'd be a fool not to admit that I am worried as well. One of them would be more than enough, but both have me very concerned. Why don't you go ahead and go to the throne for the announcement. I'll join you there in a few moments."

Reluctantly, Cian nodded and then uncurled from Mael's lap. He placed a soft kiss on Mael's lips before he stood and left. Tonight was the announcement to the court of their companionship, and a part of him couldn't help but wonder how the others would react. It was no secret, the relationship between them, but Cian knew there were those who didn't approve. Yet no amount of contempt could convince him to walk away. Mael meant everything to him. In the throne room, he stood to the back, making himself as inconspicuous as possible.

A rustle of curiosity ran through the court members as they entered the room and took their places at the tables. The sight of a carved mahogany throne to the right of Mael's, its size only slightly smaller than the prince's, signified a substantial announcement would soon be made. They both had a fair idea of the problems that would be caused by what Mael had to say, but he'd told Cian he could no longer keep silent about their relationship. To do so would taint the love Cian freely gave him, and that was something Cian kept reminding himself over and over as Mael stood before his throne. The prince held up his hand and the room became silent, all eyes fixed on him.

"As you all realize by now," Mael said, "I have chosen a companion to spend my eternity with. Tonight, I am publicly announcing my choice, so that all will know who I want beside me." It was clear that there were several in the room who were not at all happy about this; it didn't matter the name. What mattered was that it wasn't them.

Cian scanned the court members, watching their expressions closely. His heart was thundering in his chest, but no amount of thought could slow it down.

"It is with great pleasure that I announce my chosen one, Cian Carmichael." Looking over at Cian, Mael held out his hand with a soft smile. "The Romanorum has already declared the legality of my relationship with Cian."

Only a very few in the room dared to show their disdain. Some were genuinely pleased for their prince, and most wore polite, congratulatory expressions on their faces as everybody applauded. Mael's hand tightened on Cian's, drawing him against Mael's side. The contact sent a calming warmth cascading through Cian, letting him know everything was all right. As Mael sat down, he held onto Cian's hand.

Cian stifled the chuckle, noting how like his throne in Heaven this one was. Generally speaking, most of the court seemed fine, although a few made him a bit leery. A protective urge began to surface, but he pushed it away, knowing Mael was safe.

"I think that set the cat amongst the pigeons," Mael murmured while the court members began engaging in their own pursuits. "You being the cat, of course."

"I believe you're right. Although most of them are taking it better than I expected."

"Most know they had better take it well or there will be hell to pay. And I could tell a few were quite happy for us."

"Rwy'n du garu di, my sweet prince," Cian said, smiling over at Mael.

Mael drew Cian's hand up, brushing a soft kiss to the back of it. "And I believe I adore you to distraction."

Cian brushed his fingertips over Mael's lips before sliding his hand down once more. "I think maybe some are beginning to understand," he said quietly.

"They need to understand because I will tolerate no questioning of our relationship, Cian."

"If they could see within my soul, there would never be any question. We are one soul, Mael, in two bodies."

Mael nodded slowly because he did feel that. "I'm the only one allowed to see within you. The rest can go to hell," he said rather possessively.

"In so many ways, love," Cian said with a quick, discreet wink.

"I'd say in every way." Mael could very easily become jealous over the simplest thing. It thrilled Cian to no end to see that possessive side.

"I am yours and yours only, Mael. As you are only mine."

Mael's voice lowered and held a very subtle caress within the soft purr of words. "As soon as this session is over, I'd like you to show me just how much I belong to you."

Cian grinned. "You know what I would really like?"

"The pool filled with Jell-O and me having my way with you?"

Cian shook his head, giving Mael a wry grin. "No, I was thinking of a drink. Your choice as to where. My only rule: not the bedroom."

"A most excellent idea. Shall we lay a bet on how long it takes me to get you back to that bedroom?"

Cian's gaze narrowed, but he nodded. "All right, Your Excellency. You have yourself a bet. What is the wager?"

Mael stood and tugged lightly at Cian's hand to pull him up. "I think we should discuss that on our walk to the club, don't you?"

"Very well, love. After you." Cian waved his hand toward the doors.

With that regal bearing firmly in place, Mael placed Cian's hand on his arm and they strolled out of the court room together. "It's no more than a few minutes' walk to the club. Now about that wager... What would you suggest, my angel?"

"A bottle of a chosen drink and a night free to explore fantasies for the winner," Cian said. He glanced over at Mael briefly. "And for the loser, a torturous evening... with no release."

"Interesting. Then it is settled: that will be the prize. What are the rules? Shall we say, I win if it's less than an hour, and you win if it's more?"

"That works for me."

"Even without the wager, I think I will enjoy simply spending the evening with you," Mael said as they walked outside and down to the gate.

Cian pulled his hand from Mael's arm, only to slide his own arm around the prince's waist. As they continued, he relished the closeness between them. It had been a long time since he had been seated upon a throne and he still wasn't entirely used to it again. With Mael by his side, however, it was something he was more than willing to endure. At the gate, the guard quickly opened it for them, and they headed out onto the sidewalk.

"Once you get used to everything, there's probably a few things about your new position I should explain," Mael said.

"Mm," Cian mumbled softly. "Like?" He glanced over at Mael. "It's been a long time since I've been in that position and I have the feeling that being Michael's right hand differs a bit from being a prince's companion."

"Considering you aren't viewed as my right hand man, but as my hand in my absence, then yes, there is a difference. In the eyes of my court, you are me. You speak for me and your rules are to be obeyed just as much as mine are. In times of need, you can stand for me and hold sessions." Mael slid an arm around Cian's shoulder, keeping him close. Though they received a few odd stares as they walked down the street, the aura of being unapproachable deterred most from staring at them too long.

"Let them look, cariad. I am proud and honored to be by your side."

"I have no desire for their perception of their world to intrude on mine."

"True, but then, I am not from this world. So perhaps that is why it doesn't faze me. The only thing that does is the mistreatment of one's brethren. Humanity's protection is my duty." Cian rested his head lightly on Mael's shoulder as they walked. "I would like for us to spend this evening talking. About our pasts and our hopes for the future. I will hide nothing from you and I trust you to do the same."

"Then that's what we will do. Our wager can be put on hold for a later time."

"Oh, don't worry, love," Cian said as they neared the club entrance. "I never said a word about the wager being off. Perhaps we can extend the time to, say, two hours? A lot can be said... and done... within two hours."

"Or three if you wish," Mael murmured quietly before he nodded slightly to the bouncer at the door.

"Your Excellency." The large man bowed his head in respect to them.

"Three it is." Cian followed Mael through the crowd inside, watching the people around them with intense interest. It had been a while since he had felt drawn to a place like this.

The place had more of a personal club feel to it than an actual bar. A discreet, quiet ambiance filled the room. Walking inside felt akin to walking under the sea. Varying hues of green and blue colored every surface. Mermaids and sea creatures graced the walls, their shimmering bodies set off by the low green and blue lights. Several doorways led off from the main room, and a slender staircase ran along one wall to the private rooms upstairs. Drawing Cian with him, Mael led the way to one of the tables and then slid into the blue leather booth.

Cian settled on the seat across from Mael. He looked around briefly and then back to the prince. "Interesting. I take it you've frequented this place?"

"You could say... I'm a partner in the venture." Leaning forward, Mael rested his elbows on the dark wood of the table.

One of the waiters approached the table. "Good evening, Your Excellency. What can I get for you gentlemen?"

"You order?" Cian asked. "Or shall I?"

"I'll take the house special," Mael said. "You can have whatever you want, Cian. Though you might not want the house special."

Cian chuckled and looked up at the waiter. "Your best red, please." The waiter nodded before turning to head back toward the bar to fill their order. Cian looked back at Mael. "Dare I ask what the house special is?"

The prince smirked. "I'm a vampire. Do you really need to ask?"

"Smart ass."

"I try my best and it's encouraging to know I'm succeeding." The slow smile that eased over Mael's lips had a wicked touch to it.

A moment later, the waiter returned. Placing the wine in front of Cian, the man gave him a friendly smile before setting Mael's glass down. Bowing to both of them, the waiter left.

Cian rolled his eyes playfully and glanced down into his wine. "Would you do something for me, love?" he asked as he allowed the illusion hiding his wings to falter for a brief moment. He reached behind him and plucked a feather. The wing faded from sight.

Mael watched him curiously. "What do you want?"

Cian pressed the feather between his fingers, focused his gaze on it, and slid his fingers slowly up the length. As he passed over the silky surface, the shimmering blue gave way to stainless steel. He looked back at Mael and smiled. "Give me your hand?"

"There are rooms upstairs if you want me to feed you." Mael held out his hand, palm up.

"I only wish to sweeten the wine." Cian took Mael's hand in his and drew the blade of the knife over Mael's palm, creating a two-inch cut. He turned Mael's hand over, letting the blood flow into the wine. A few seconds later, he turned it back over and slid his own hand over Mael's palm, healing the wound. He raised the blade to his lips and licked Mael's blood from the steel before blowing on it. The illusion faded and a feather floated down to the tabletop. "Thank you."

Remaining quiet, Mael watched Cian. "Too early for any kind of privacy?"

Cian lifted the glass and took a slow sip, shuddering as the taste of Mael's blood hit him. "Much too early, love," he said with a wink as he set the glass back down.

Picking up his own glass, Mael took a drink, his gaze never leaving Cian's. "It does taste better directly from the source, you know."

"I haven't tried hard enough to drive you insane yet."

"Now what is it you want to talk about?" Mael asked, settling back into the booth seat.

"Quid pro quo. You start. Ask me anything."

"For starters, I find myself curious about your existence as an angel. Though I wouldn't know where to begin with the questions. So simply start where you want and tell me about your life."

"Ah, yes," Cian said with a nod. "Very well. I was created nearly three thousand years ago by the Archangel Michael. In essence, I am his son, although all angels could be considered as such. As an angel, I was born as you see me now, though not as strong and with less power. That developed over time. I was appointed to be his right hand, to sit beside him in his palace. I am one of his commanders and fought alongside him during the battle of Lucifer's fall. Several hundred years ago, I volunteered to be sent to Earth, to keep watch over humanity." Cian took a drink and glanced up at Mael. "And now for you. Where are you from? Where were you born?"

With a slight movement of his hand, Mael insured their conversation went no further than the two of them. "I was born a free citizen of Rome a very long time ago. A lot longer ago than the majority know. Off the record, I was born in 20 AD; on the record, I was born in 1329." He paused, as if considering his next question to ask. "How many have you loved, Cian?"

Cian smiled. "Aside from you, I have only loved one other. His name was Richard and he was a knight during the Second Crusade. I was the one who found him after his final battle. I was too late to help him and he died in my arms. He was the last I ever made love to, before you came along. And you?"

Mael sighed quietly, a more introspective look appearing on his face. "I have loved three others, and most unsuccessfully. Or I thought I did. Now I'm not quite sure. Cornelius was one, and another was one of my Children, Amael. In him, I hadn't chosen wisely at all, and it became necessary to reclaim the blood I gave him. The last was when I was mortal, and I never knew his name. Sometimes my soul feels older than it really is." He chuckled softly. "When you first met me, what were your thoughts?"

"Before I brought Brandon to you, I wanted to make sure I was making the right decision. Therefore, I spied on you. I watched you during a court session and later with Seth. I think maybe it was that night that I fell in love with you. After that night, your face and your voice haunted me. I wanted you, with all my heart and soul." Cian sighed and took a drink, staring down into his wine. "Mael, once an angel loves, it becomes a lifeline. To lose it would be akin to death." He looked up at the prince. "Now what about you? What were your initial thoughts?"

Mael covered Cian's hand as he listened. "Unfortunately not as pure as yours. You haunted me after the first time I saw you as well. Somehow, my thoughts didn't quite seem my own anymore and they constantly strayed toward you. You remind me of sunshine and warmth."

"Your love is the force that keeps me going," Cian said quietly. "I know it's there." He caught Mael's hand in his own, bringing it to his lips to press a soft kiss on the top. "I love you," he whispered against it. "What is your next question for me?"

"In a way, I think I already know what I want to know about you, Cian. I have the most important parts of you. To know that your love for me has become life to you... Why don't you just tell me what you want me to know?"

"I've told you everything I can think of. Except..." Cian looked at a point somewhere over Mael's shoulder, lost in thought for a brief moment. "I cannot die, except by dark magic. And even then, it is a temporary death. My body would return to Heaven, where the poison from the magic would be removed. How long that takes depends on the strength of the magic." His grip on Mael's hand tightened. "I wanted to tell you that, should something ever happen to me. I don't want to risk leaving you with no knowledge of what's going on."

Mael nodded slowly. "You've lived longer than I have, Cian. I think we are both rather hardy creatures. I do have one other question for you. What about this Zalael? I'm not that informed when it comes to demons. So how powerful is this one?"

"Zalael was one of the strongest demons I've had to banish from this plane. It wasn't long after Richard died that a young sorcerer summoned Zalael. In order to move about undetected in this world, Zalael had to have a human body as a vehicle." Cian sighed and ran the fingers of his other hand through his hair. A few moments of silence passed before he could continue. "I no longer remember the sorcerer's name, but Michael had warned me about Zalael before I finally met him face to face. No matter the mental preparations I put myself through, I still was not ready to see him. He succeeded in killing me, and only after my resurrection was I able to banish him. He is only a few steps below Lucifer himself, Mael. He was created by Lucifer."

"It helps to know what we might be facing, but I think I'd rather talk about us instead. You are, after all, my first companion, something I think I am going to enjoy getting used to."

"Aye, cariad." Cian rubbed his thumb over the top of Mael's hand. "So does this mean we are married?" he asked with soft chuckle.

"In the vampire society version, it is pretty much the same; so yes, we are. Not a state I ever wanted to share with another. Cornelius never wanted it, and Amael wanted it only for the extra power it would give him." Mael shrugged. "However, we are bound for eternity, and the Romanorum has no divorce court."

"Good. Because I'll be damned if you could ever get rid of me." Cian flashed Mael a wicked grin. "Tell me, love. Do you dance?"

"And here I was going to take great pleasure in informing you that you're stuck with me." Arching a brow at the question, Mael said, "Of course I dance. Are you asking me to?"

"You might have the opportunity to take your pleasure later," Cian remarked as he got up. He held out a hand to Mael. "For now, I want to see you dance. I haven't danced in several hundred years and even then it was for a sheik."

"Later I want you to dance for me just as you did for a sheik, my angel," Mael murmured. Taking hold of Cian's hand, he slid out of the booth. Once close enough, Mael leaned in to press a soft kiss to Cian's lips. "I want your promise that I'll get to see it."

"Oh, believe me, love, you will. Lead the way."

Arousal lit Mael's eyes as he stepped back. He led Cian silently toward one of the closed doors, then opened it. A smaller bar lined one wall, and the atmosphere had a more intimate feel as other couples danced closely together on the dance floor. The low, sensual throb of the music stirred over Cian's senses. Bypassing the bar, Cian took the lead, pulling the prince out into the middle of the dance floor. He turned and slipped an arm around Mael's waist, pressing their bodies together lightly as he began to move.

"Muscle control," he whispered on Mael's lips, "is one of the first things they teach you. To isolate the muscle groups of your body, until you can control each one alone." From the hips down, he swayed, the serpentine movements causing their bodies to brush repeatedly. "It's like a watching a snake dance."

Mael settled his hands on Cian's hips, the light touch of their bodies definitely affecting him if the hardness Cian felt was any indication. "Keep that up and you'll not have your evening out, my angel." Mael had that look in his eyes that told Cian exactly what the prince wanted to do to him.

Cian pulled away slowly. Free of Mael's grip, he closed his eyes and began to lose himself in the feel of the music. Before long, the music in his mind took over, and his body moved to it, an ancient, Eastern rhythm that drew out the serpent's moves, as he'd learned so long ago. Each muscle in his body moved exactly how he wished, the sway of his hips becoming a means of weaving a spell of seduction on his prince. "Possess me."

Without warning, Mael's hands were on him, hauling Cian against a hard body as shadows descended over them. In the darkness, a hard, devouring kiss took Cian's breath away. His hands fell to the prince's hips, and he broke the kiss long enough to lick first at one fang and then the other. His tongue caressed the curve of the sharp tooth, and his grip tightened on Mael's hips.

"Take me. Show me how much I belong to you, prince. Leave no inch of my body unmarked by you."

The teasing licks to his fangs caused a deep, rumbling growl to emerge in Mael, and the tip of a tooth nicked into Cian's tongue. The heated flavor of the angel's blood tinged their kiss. When the shadows dissolved around them, they were standing in their bedroom. Several tendrils of shadow that didn't fade took on solid shape and the edges of them sharpened. The shadows slid beneath clothing, leaving nothing but ribbons of cloth to fall to the floor.

Cian backed away and reclined on the bed. Raising his arms to rest on the pillow above his head, he locked his fingers together. "I am yours. Do with me what you will."

Mael followed Cian onto the bed and crawled between his legs, nudging them wider apart. The sensation of skin on skin, their cocks grazing one another, sent shivers through Cian. He opened his legs more, and Mael's cock pushed downward, the head nudging Cian's entrance. "If I did that," Mael said, rocking his hips, "I would hurt you."

Cian reached up and gripped Mael's head tightly. He flicked his tongue over Mael's fangs again, knowing damn well the reaction he would get. "I want you to." He wrapped his legs around Mael's waist, thrusting his hips up. "Now, Mael," he growled as his head tilted back.

As one hand turned Cian's head, Mael struck quickly, sinking his fangs deep. A sudden, hard, driving force impaled Cian in one thrust, and he cried out, arching his back and thrusting his hips up to meet Mael. His hands fell to the prince's shoulders and then slid down Mael's back, raking his fingernails across Mael's skin. A shockwave ruptured inside him and he gripped Mael tightly as his body shook violently beneath the prince. The hard, hungry pull at his throat sent fresh shocks through him. With a final cry, his orgasm fully hit him, flooding the connection between them as his body rocked and tears spilled down his cheeks.

Mael thrust harder and faster until the tight strain of his hips kept him buried deep inside Cian as he continued drinking hungrily. Heat suddenly flooded Cian's body, taking his breath away. For the briefest second, the room around them lit up, pulsing with a blinding light, before it died away. Cian slid his arms around Mael's shoulders, unable to stop the shaking. Mael's face remained pressed against Cian's throat as the prince's body went completely rigid for a long moment. Only when it faded did Mael collapse on him.

Cian squeezed his eyes shut as he struggled to regain his breath. When he finally found his voice, it was hoarse. "I have no idea what that was."

"I am inside you," Mael whispered, sounding as much in awe as Cian felt. "Not just... physically, Cian."

"I am you." In the quiet stillness of the room, the only sound that could be heard was Cian's ragged breath.

It took several minutes before either of them could move. Mael took a deep, steadying breath and eased out, rolling slowly onto his side. Cian nestled close, slipping an arm around Mael's waist.

"I love you so much," he whispered. He nuzzled Mael's neck softly, still completely lost in the moment.

"I've never felt anything like what I feel with you." One hand slipped beneath Cian's chin to raise his face to meet Mael's stunned gaze.

Cian smiled up at him. "Your soul is my life. Without it, I could not go on."

"I was inside your soul."

Cian shook his head. "You were not inside my soul, my prince." He propped himself up on his forearm and leaned over Mael. "You *are* my soul."

Chapter Six

Brandon settled back on his stool, returning to his book after straightening things up. It was the third time he'd read the book and he never got tired of it. Just as Brandon started reading, Cornelius shuffled into the workroom, his robe looking like he'd slept in it. Brandon knew the mage had been somewhat preoccupied, but then Cornelius always got like that when he thought he was about to make a major breakthrough on one of his rituals.

Brandon cocked an eyebrow at him. "You look like you had an interesting rest," he said with a chuckle.

Lifting his hand to adjust his spectacles, Cornelius peered at Brandon over the rims. "Rest? Oh, yes, I didn't get much of that." He hurried over to the work table and grabbed his notepad. For a few moments, he scribbled on it in silence, frowning fiercely in his concentration.

Brandon watched him curiously, waiting until Cornelius stopped writing before speaking again. "It was so cool to hear Mael make the announcement about his relationship with Cian," Brandon muttered, going back to his book to hide the slight scowl.

"I don't doubt his ability to squelch any objections to the fact he's chosen Cian as his companion," Cornelius murmured as he continued writing. "Probably not the wisest thing Mael has done, but they'll manage."

Brandon closed his book abruptly and stood. "It must be nice to be able to express their love openly," he said bitterly. He shoved his hands into the pockets of his jeans and looked around the work room. "So what do you want me to do tonight?"

"You are bothered."

Brandon shrugged. "A bit, I suppose." He looked down and fingered the binding of his book. "I know it's ridiculous to be and I don't begrudge them that. I just..." He sighed and closed his eyes. "Nothing," he said quietly. "I didn't mean to interrupt you if you were busy. What do you need me to do tonight?"

Cornelius set his pencil down and reached out, pulling Brandon to him. "It's times like these I don't really know what to say, Brandon. I can't help thinking you'd be better off with someone else."

"And lose what I have with you?" Brandon looked up at him and smiled wistfully. "I can't imagine not loving you, Cornelius."

Cornelius' arms settled around his waist, drawing Brandon in tighter. "If I could, I would give you everything you wanted. You know that, don't you?"

"All I want is your heart, Cornelius." Brandon traced his fingertip over Cornelius' chest softly. "So long as you love me, that's all I need."

"But you want and need more. I don't blame you. For the first time in my life, I want it all, just as you do." Leaning forward slightly, Cornelius pressed a soft kiss to Brandon's lips.

"I can't live without you," Brandon murmured.

Brandon's hold around Cornelius' neck tightened and his lips parted. His tongue snaked out to take a taste of the mage's lips, and he shuddered in Cornelius' arms as a small gasp escaped him. The hold around him tightened as Cornelius slowly drew Brandon's tongue in, deepening the kiss.

For a moment, Brandon lost himself before pulling slowly away. He took a deep, steadying breath. As he rested his forehead against the mage's, he groaned. "I want you," he whispered, "so fucking bad." The feel of their bodies pressed together brought images to his mind of him beneath Cornelius. It was enough to draw another frustrated groan from him.

"Why don't we go relax tonight, instead of working?"

Brandon nodded and stepped back reluctantly. "Your room or mine?"

"I think mine tonight." Cornelius didn't say anything else as he headed for the door. He stayed silent on their way down the stairs and to his bedroom.

Brandon walked into the room and sat down on the bed. "What did you have in mind for tonight?"

After closing the door, Cornelius joined Brandon on the bed. Leaning against the headboard to get more comfortable, he said, "I thought we could talk for a time. I enjoy it when you share your thoughts with me."

Brandon lay across the end of the bed, putting his arms under his head. "Anything in particular?"

Cornelius slid further down, rolling to his side next to Brandon. "Anything you would like to talk about." Cornelius' hand hovered above Brandon, a soft touch straying over the front of his shirt.

Brandon closed his eyes and smiled wistfully. "I remember the first time I discovered alchemy. I was seven. I found some old books of my grandfather's in our attic. I found out later that he had been a Freemason and was intensely interested in alchemy. That's where my copy of The Forge and the Crucible came from. I remember reading through those books and even back then I couldn't put them down."

Resting a hand against Brandon's chest where his heart once beat, Cornelius listened silently. Brandon moved one of his hands and slid it over Cornelius', then continued. "I first discovered magic when I joined a coven when I was thirteen. It was just a group of friends, what few I had, and we did simple stuff, like levitation and things like that. It wasn't until a couple of years ago, during my time on the streets, that I experienced what I would call real magic. I was lying on a park bench one day, wondering where I was going to go that night. I opened my eyes and looked up at the clouds. There was a guy's face, I kid you not, formed in the clouds. It was an old friend of mine. A few hours later, he found me in a bar and offered me his spare room for a while. It was unbelievable."

"Not so strange. Sometimes magic can come to us when we need it most." Cornelius leaned over, the soft brush of his lips touching Brandon's cheek. His hand slid lower, coming to rest against Brandon's stomach.

The muscles in Brandon's belly tightened, and he nodded slowly. "Yes," he whispered. He turned his head and brushed their lips together.

"I don't know how long I will be allowed to have you," the mage whispered. "But in that time, I want all of you that I can have."

Brandon's response died out in their kiss. His hand snaked beneath Cornelius' hair to cup the back of Cornelius' head. He pulled the mage down, deepening their kiss. He wanted more than anything to feel Cornelius' touch, any way he could. Edging up underneath the bottom of his shirt, Cornelius' hand caressed the bare skin of Brandon's stomach. A soft moan escaped Brandon, and he caught Cornelius' tongue, sucking on it gently. His other hand played absently with the raven curls, curling them around his fingers before letting them slip free. With the mage's touch, he shifted closer, their bodies pressing together.

Cornelius lowered his hand to the button of Brandon's pants, undoing them slowly. As he broke off the kiss, he slid the pants down Brandon's hips. "I had wanted things to be slow with you, but I don't think my good intentions will last."

Brandon lifted his hips to allow Cornelius to slide his jeans off. At the same moment, Brandon reached down, cupping Cornelius through his robe, whispering, "I need you." Then he sat up, pulling his shirt over his head. "Your turn."

Cornelius' gaze roamed over Brandon as the mage unzipped his robe. He rose up and slid the garment off, and Brandon moved closer. He ran his fingers over Cornelius' chest and leaned forward. With the tip of his tongue, he circled Cornelius' left nipple before closing his mouth over it. He flicked it with his tongue, then suckled on it gently.

Cornelius' hand cradled Brandon's head against him. "You've a very sweet mouth."

"And it's all yours," Brandon murmured against the mage's chest. He pulled away and kissed a slow path up, until he was on his knees as well. He snaked his arms around Cornelius' neck and gasped as their bodies pressed together. "Everything I have is yours, love."

"I'm going to take everything you are as mine. That I promise you."

"Please," Brandon whispered on Cornelius' lips.

Cornelius pressed Brandon gently back onto the bed and then hovered over him as he scattered light kisses along Brandon's chest. Lifting his head, Cornelius slicked his hand, then slowly rubbed his cock. His gaze held Brandon's with a fierce intensity that rivaled anything the mage did in the workroom. The knowledge that Cornelius wanted him left Brandon aching. The deep emerald of the mage's eyes took on a heated blaze as Brandon opened his legs, allowing Cornelius to settle between them. His hands drifted over the mage's shoulders to cup Cornelius' neck on either side.

Cornelius' hips nudged closer and the tip of his cock pushed gently in against Brandon's hole. As Cornelius surged into him, Brandon gasped, eyes going wide, back arching. He dug his fingers into Cornelius' shoulders, entire body shaking as the mage's cock filled him.

"Oh God..."

Rocking his hips up, he met every one of Cornelius' thrusts. He circled Cornelius' waist with his legs, allowing Cornelius to go deeper. Within that emerald gaze, he saw himself reflected, and it was that thought that finally brought the tears to his eyes. As his body began to tighten, he kept his eyes open. He shuddered beneath Cornelius, unable to hold himself back any longer. As he slipped over the edge, the tears fell as the mage's name slipped from his lips.

"Brandon..." Cornelius groaned, strokes quickening, hips rocking until he froze, soul bared in his eyes as he came.

Brandon clung tightly, his body still shaking. The knowledge of the bond between them settled over him, blanketing him in a love that was soul-deep. This hadn't been about sex—he wasn't sure it ever was. Only when he began to come down did the weight of what they had done hit Brandon. It made him cling tighter to Cornelius, truly afraid to let the mage go. What if Mael found out?

"To tell you that I love you doesn't seem enough," Brandon whispered against the raven curls brushing his face. He sighed and closed his eyes. "It's something much deeper, more than I ever thought possible."

"Once given life, emotions in us take on their own depth. I know you more than others, just as you do me."

Brandon swallowed hard and buried his face in Cornelius' hair. When he spoke, his voice was quiet. "I would bring down the heavens for you if I could," he whispered. "I can't begin to explain how much you mean to me."

"There are no words for it, Brandon. Simply feel."

Brandon's hold tightened around Cornelius as he nuzzled Cornelius' neck softly. His tongue darted out to take a taste, drawing a shudder up his spine. He felt the mage in his mind, the connection strengthened more than he ever thought possible. What was done, he couldn't undo—never intended to. With another slow flick of his tongue, Brandon opened his mouth, sinking his fangs into Cornelius' throat. He whimpered softly as he fed. A soft sigh escaped Cornelius, the sound pure bliss. When Brandon had taken enough, he licked the wound to close it. He slid his fingers through Cornelius' hair and lifted the mage's head up. He teased soft lips, then along the mage's fangs. Then he pulled Cornelius down into a slow, searing kiss, the flavor of his blood sweetening it.

Cornelius' hands slid down over Brandon's sides, resting at his hips. When the kiss ended, Brandon smiled and reached up to trace fingertips over Cornelius' cheek, along his jaw, and finally across his lips. Brandon loved to touch this man, just to feel the softness of his skin. It wasn't a sexual exploration, just quiet adoration. Simply from the look in the mage's eyes, Brandon knew he didn't need to say anything. Every thought was open to the mage, and Brandon knew Cornelius read him like an open book. Cornelius caught Brandon's hand, brought it to his lips, and pressed a kiss to each finger. What they had done, this connection between them, couldn't be undone, except by death.

* * *

Back to work, looking none the worse for wear and a bit more rested, Sav listened while Mael muttered, pacing back and forth before dropping down onto his desk chair. "Only three people entered the grounds at the time, Sav. All of them were normal deliveries and none of the men even entered the palace itself. How the hell did that rose get here?"

"It's somebody in the palace, Your Excellency. I'm certain of that."

"All of the lower level employees have been interrogated." Opening his drawer, Mael drew out the memory orb and handed it to her. "Go over it, see if I missed anything. Everybody shows up clean."

"I think the better question is: who wasn't questioned? That would be a good starting point."

Mael frowned at her inference, but couldn't argue with it. It was more likely their problem was somebody in a higher position. The real question was just how close to him the trouble was. "That is the same conclusion I've come to."

Before he could say more, the office door opened and Selena poised in the doorway. Her expression held a wicked edge to it, just as it always did when she was about to start her own brand of trouble. Her head was turned, looking further down the hallway at something Mael couldn't see.

"Well, well, how intriguing," she purred.

"I would say the same." A soft chuckle followed the words, and Mael recognized his Son's voice.

Sav sat silently in her seat with a smile that told Mael she was enjoying the general aggravation he was about to undergo.

"Thanks for the support, Sav," he grumbled.

Sav smirked at him as Selena and Christian came into his office.

"Father, where have you been hiding this beautiful creature?" With a slow smile, Christian's gaze swept over Selena. In response, the titian-haired witch viewed Christian under her lashes with her own smile.

"She's taken, Christian. Which, in this case, means hands completely off." Mael had no desire for a vengeful Archangel wreaking havoc on his Son.

"That doesn't mean I can't enjoy the view." Selena stepped closer to Christian, resting her hand on the front of his shirt. In the next instant, she stiffened suddenly.

Mael laughed. "You know, Selena, Michael must work overtime on those little reminders to you." Christian looked between them both, completely puzzled. "Michael would be... " Mael trailed off, trying to find an appropriate word to insert. "Michael is her Master, and he's given to sending her reminders when she gets out of hand." The word was one Christian would understand, though it earned Mael a scowl from Selena.

"Ah, what a pity." Christian drew her hand to his lips. He kissed the back of it, then released her.

"Did you want something, Selena?" Mael asked pointedly.

"Cornelius wanted to meet with you and asked me to be here." Shrugging, Selena sat down in a chair in front of Mael's desk.

"And you?" he asked, eyeing his Son.

"I just wanted to talk with you, Father. The undercurrent of tension in this place is beyond noticeable."

"Oh, good, you're already here." Cornelius breezed into the room with his normal manner, giving Selena a smile before he turned his attention to Mael.

Addressing his Son, Mael said quietly, "That is because we are under attack. Sav, go ahead and fill Christian in while I talk with Cornelius and Selena."

Sav stood and walked over to Christian. Cornelius took her seat and quickly filled Mael in. "Selena and I have come up with a few options in dealing with Zalael and Memnet. Unfortunately, both require close proximity."

"Then I will take Zalael while you deal with Memnet," Mael said.

"But—" Selena interrupted him and, in turn, Mael raised his hand, silencing her.

"You are not going to be in the middle of it, Selena. Not if I can help it, and I doubt if Michael will allow you anywhere near Memnet."

Selena glared at him, but remained silent.

"If you could borrow the Sword of Michael again, it would be most helpful, Mael," Cornelius continued as if they hadn't been interrupted. "At least against Memnet."

"Since neither of us can wield it, Cian will have to discuss that with Michael." As much as he preferred to keep Cian out of it, Mael knew it wouldn't be possible this time.

"I'm catching occasional demonic pulses from the shipping district, but nothing to pinpoint an exact location, and it's been impossible to trace Memnet," Cornelius said, sounding as frustrated as Mael felt.

With the lull, Selena stepped in. "I've felt Memnet close by a few times, but never for very long, Mael."

"Nor am I any closer to finding out who in the palace is betraying us," Mael muttered. The situation was escalating, their position too vulnerable to be this clueless.

"I have a few ideas on that one, Your Excellency," Sav broke in. "I'm also keeping a very careful eye on them."

Mael gave her a grateful nod before she turned to leave the room. Both Selena and Cornelius stood at the same time to follow her out. Near the door, Selena paused, looking back at Mael.

"We'll track them down, Mael. I have faith in all of you, and I know it's not misplaced."

Her vote of confidence in him momentarily surprised Mael. After everybody left, he turned to his Son. His smile took on a rueful edge, catching the look on Christian's face.

"I know you too well, Mael. You are trying to take it all on yourself and always act as if you have everything perfectly under control."

Mael got up and walked around the desk, then stilled near his Son. "Because I do have everything taken care of."

"Liar." Christian said the one word softly before he added, "You're not getting away with that this time, old man. You do have people close enough who know you better than that. You can drop the facade. You should have told me sooner."

The last thing Mael wanted was his own Son involved in the middle of all the danger. "No, Christian, you will stay out of this one. You know very well there is nothing I can't handle."

"It's been a very long time since you've told me what I can and can't do. I'm as likely to listen now as I listened then." Christian took Mael's hand and tugged, drawing Mael closer.

"The fewer people who get hurt in this, the happier I will be."

"But I happen to know somebody who was once a member of Memnet's little club, Mael. It's no hardship to ask a few questions, and it's not exactly putting myself in the line of fire."

Staring at him, Mael could easily see the emotions behind what his Son was doing. There was no doubt how much Christian adored him; Mael had always known that. Their problems lay in other directions. "Then ask your questions and keep yourself out of the middle of it."

Chapter Seven

Cornelius had a problem perfecting his latest enchantment. The spell was supposed to imbue weapons with the potential for magical damage, but he wasn't getting anywhere with it. Glancing over at Brandon, he smiled despite his frustration. It never ceased to amaze him, having somebody beside him in all of this.

Brandon looked up from the notes he'd been scribbling and set his pen down. He turned on his stool and leaned to the side, elbow propped on the table. "I love watching you work."

"Right now, you're seeing a very frustrated sorcerer," Cornelius muttered, turning back to his work.

Brandon slipped a hand under Cornelius' chin, lifting his head up to meet Brandon's gaze. "Frustrated or no, I still love to watch you. Anything I can do, babe?"

Cornelius blinked, gaze lowering to Brandon's mouth. "Kiss me?"

Brandon smiled and slid his hand around Cornelius' neck to pull him closer. "You can have a kiss anytime you want it, love," he whispered. He licked Cornelius' lips slowly before parting them with his tongue, slipping it into Cornelius' mouth.

Cornelius moaned softly as he sucked on Brandon's tongue. This was one of the fringe benefits of having Brandon with him, and he adored the distraction. Without breaking their kiss, Brandon stood and moved closer, standing between Cornelius' legs, arms around Cornelius' neck. Breaking off the kiss finally, Cornelius moved lower, nuzzling Brandon's throat.

"Doesn't look like much work is getting done," he murmured.

Brandon threaded his fingers through Cornelius' hair. "It will," he whispered. "Eventually. Please..."

Cornelius knew what Brandon wanted and his fangs sank into the soft skin in answer. He tightened his mouth and drank deeply, savoring that taste of his lover. One of his legs circled to the back of the young vampire's, drawing Brandon's body in closer to him.

"Cornelius..." His name fell from Brandon's lips as a soft whisper. Brandon cupped the back of his head, holding him close, as his lover's other hand slid down Cornelius' back, fingertips tracing a soft line down Cornelius' spine to his waist.

Brandon moaned softly and turned them, leaning back against the table and pulling Cornelius against him. "I love you so much." Brandon pushed Cornelius' hair away from his neck and froze suddenly. "Oh God..."

Feeling Brandon stiffen, it took Cornelius a second to realize something was very wrong. Turning his head quickly, he saw the one person who didn't need to see this. There was no mistaking the dark anger on Mael's face. "Mael—"

"If you two are finished, I want to talk to you, Cornelius."

Cornelius' arms tightened around Brandon. "I know you do, Your Excellency. I will explain everything."

Brandon shook his head slowly. "Mael, please..."

Cornelius silenced Brandon with a finger, giving him a soft kiss. "Let me talk to Mael, Brandon. Why don't you go to your room for now?"

Tears began to fill Brandon's eyes. "No," he whispered. "I can't leave you, Cornelius."

"Shush, Child, it will only make him angrier. Let me talk to him." Cornelius released him, watching with dread as Brandon slipped out the door. Sighing, he looked back at Mael. "It isn't as you think, Mael."

"Then what would it be? You've obviously forgotten yourself so far as to involve Brandon in something that should never touch him." Mael had a temper, but Cornelius had never seen him so angry that the prince's words were hissed between clenched teeth. "How far has this gone?"

"He is my Child, Mael."

Mael grabbed Cornelius and slammed him against the wall. "What will happen to Brandon when your magic takes precedence over him?" he snarled. "Does his heart break while you putter around in your workroom, barely paying attention? You knew not to touch him and yet you disobeyed me!"

"It is not like what happened between me and you! Or any of the others. I swear." Cornelius refused to back down on this. He owed it to both himself and to Brandon to stand his ground.

Mael growled at him and released him abruptly. "I've nursed enough broken hearts when it comes to you, Cornelius." Before Cornelius could say a word, Mael continued, "You will leave now and go to your estate. Do not leave there until I tell you otherwise."

Cornelius' eyes widened in shock as Mael whirled around and left the room. Cornelius stood frozen, devastated by the thought of never seeing Brandon again. He had to leave, he knew he had to. If he didn't, Mael would have him forcibly removed. Numbly, he turned to look at the table, staring at it helplessly. Finally, he forced his feet to move and he left the room, leaving everything untouched.

* * *

Brandon paced the floor restlessly, fighting the urge to sneak back to the workroom and listen through the door. The anger in Mael's eyes had been painfully obvious, and Brandon was beyond terrified. When a knock sounded at his bedroom door, his stomach twisted, knowing it was the last person he wanted to see.

"What do you want?" Brandon grumbled as Mael walked in. "Where the fuck is Cornelius?"

"Cornelius has been sent to his own estate, Brandon. He knew better than to start anything with you."

Brandon stopped pacing then. He spun around and glared at Mael. "What? What right do you have to dictate whom he loves?"

"Brandon, Cornelius knew when he took you on to train that any emotional entanglement wouldn't last. He's always become lost in his magic and nothing will ever change that. Too many have already been hurt before."

"Bullshit, Mael!" Brandon banged his fist against the post of his bed. "I've taken the time to get to know him, as he has me. You know nothing about him if you think he's a shallow man with no heart." He stormed over to his closet and flung it open, looking for his leather jacket.

"I never said he didn't have a heart, Brandon, and I know very well he never intends to hurt anybody. I've known him for too many centuries," Mael said with infuriating calm.

"You know nothing," Brandon said bitterly as he jerked his jacket off its hanger. "I suppose you never intend to hurt anyone either."

"How am I supposed to answer that?" With a sigh, Mael opened the door again and left the room without another word.

Brandon slammed his fist into the wall. Heedless of the tears as they streamed down his face, he pulled his jacket on. When Cornelius' scent reached him through the leather, Brandon fell back against the wall with a sound that was half-growl and half-scream. Steeling himself, he pushed away and headed down the stairs, not bothering to stop by the throne room to tell anyone where he was going. Fuck him! Fuck Mael Black and his self-righteous bullshit, Brandon fumed silently as he threw open the front door.

He stepped out into the rain and took great care to slam the door behind him. He shoved his hands into his pockets and headed down to the gate. The guard nodded and let him through. Once he stepped out into the street, Brandon started walking toward the city. He didn't know where he was going. In truth, he no longer cared. Despite the rage and pain, he felt empty.

Nothing mattered anymore. He found his way to the nearest pub, went in, and dropped onto a stool at the bar.

"What'll you have?"

"Whiskey," Brandon muttered without looking up. A few minutes later a shot of whiskey was set in front of him. He tipped his head back and downed the alcohol, wincing slightly with the burn. When a hand touched his shoulder, he nearly jumped out of his skin, hand raised to strike.

"Whoa!"

A strong grip wrapped tightly around Brandon's wrist. He looked up then. "Cian."

Cian gave Brandon a worried look as he sat down. "What's wrong?"

"Your prince," Brandon said bitterly as he waved at the bartender. He started to dig more money out of his pocket, but Cian stopped him. Brandon watched as Cian handed the bartender money and the bottle was left in front of them. Cian poured more whiskey into Brandon's glass.

"What has Mael done?" Cian asked as he capped the bottle and set it back down.

"He walked in on us, Cian. Cornelius and I were in the workroom. Mael saw us kissing."

Cian groaned. "Oh, no." He looked over as Brandon drank the whiskey in the glass before pouring more. "And Cornelius?"

"The bastard banished him." Brandon downed his shot and slammed the glass down hard. "The son of a bitch took away the man I love!"

"When was the last time you fed?"

Brandon looked up at him. "Why?"

"I've been around vampires enough to know when one of them hasn't fed in some time."

Brandon sighed and stared down at the bar. "It's been a while, I would've fed..." He fell silent and shook his head.

"Come."

Cian stood and pulled Brandon from his stool, despite Brandon's protests. Brandon followed behind, letting Cian lead him out of the pub. Brandon wondered briefly where they were going, but then the familiar sight of the hotel run by St. Mary's came into view and he stopped. Cian stopped as well and looked back at him.

"Brandon."

"No, Cian. I don't want to feed."

Cian tugged on his arm again. "Don't make me force you, Brandon."

Brandon scowled, but as it always seemed to be with Cian, any touch of anger dissipated when the angel's gaze held him so intently. "Cian, please. I just..." Brandon sighed and looked off into the distance. "I don't want to go on. Not without Cornelius."

Cian stepped close to him, releasing Brandon's arm to cup his face gently. "I will not let you harm yourself, Brandon. Cornelius would never forgive me."

Brandon blinked once and the tears began to fall again. "I can't live without him," he whispered.

"I know. Mael will come to his senses. I have faith in him." Cian pressed a soft kiss to Brandon's lips. "And I have faith in the love between you and Cornelius. It will survive Mael's wrath."

"Please..." It was all Brandon could say. He had tasted Cian's blood before; he knew it could end the hunger within him. And for a short time, he knew it would ease the pain as well.

"Come with me. I will do what I can," Cian said.

Brandon offered no protest. He wanted the hunger gone. He wanted to stop hurting, at least for the moment. He followed Cian up the stairwell and to the second floor. As soon as Cian opened the door to the room he kept and walked inside, Brandon closed it behind them and shoved Cian against the wall, fangs bared and hunger boiling to the surface. Cian simply wrapped his arms around Brandon and tipped his head in invitation. Brandon sank his fangs into Cian's throat, groaning as the sweet, rich blood spilled over his tongue. He molded his body to Cian's, fighting the natural reactions that wanted much more than blood. Cian would never agree to anything more, and, in truth, neither could Brandon.

When he knew he had taken enough, Brandon licked the wound closed and rested his head on Cian's shoulder, breaking down in tears. Cian held him close and kissed his hair softly while murmuring whispers of reassurance.

* * *

Mael sat brooding in the throne room after he'd dismissed everyone. The room darkened, lit only by a few torches along the walls. Closing his eyes, he rested his head back against the seat. He was beyond hurt that Cornelius had betrayed not only him, but had dragged Brandon into it as well. Too many times he'd watched as others thought to capture the enigmatic magician for themselves. Hell, he had been deeply in love with Cornelius himself a long time ago. He knew the pain when the realization set in that magic was the all-important thing to Cornelius, and he'd seen the realization in too many other eyes. Mael didn't want to see that look in Brandon's eyes when it began to dawn on the young man that no matter how much he loved the magician, it wasn't enough.

"Have you lost your mind?"

Mael didn't open his eyes. "I've already heard enough about it from them."

"Then you will hear it again from me," Cian said. "Do you have any idea what you've done, Mael?"

"I am protecting Brandon, Cian. That is what I am doing."

"You have broken his heart," Cian shot back. "Who are you to choose who he loves? Who are you to choose who Cornelius loves?"

Mael's eyes flew open, anger barely held in check. "I am the one who protects Brandon! Regardless of anything else, I will not have that Child hurt. And he will be, sooner or later. Cornelius knew better than to even go that far with one so young."

"Has it not occurred to you that you have hurt him more than anyone ever could?" Cian snapped.

"Has it never occurred to you why I would take such a drastic action if I didn't believe there were a fucking damn good reason, Cian?" Mael shouted, fingers digging into the arms of his throne.

"I have spent the past several hours forcing Brandon to feed from me because he was ready to die!" Cian leaned forward, gripping both arms of the throne tightly, face within inches of Mael's. "Perhaps it would be clearer if you were to put us in their place. I would die without you. And Brandon is ready to die without Cornelius. Their souls were bound long before now. Or have you forgotten that I have the ability to see that?" He straightened back up, turning away from Mael. "Their love runs deep," he said quietly. "As a Father and Child. As lovers. They are one soul in two bodies. Sound familiar?"

A white hot rage tore through Mael with the comparison to what he and Cian had, and he opened his mouth to say something he knew he'd regret. In a concerted effort to keep the words back, he ended up biting savagely into his own lip. Lifting a hand, he wiped away the trickle of blood. He was acutely aware when Cian purposely ignored the scent, so much so that it made him ache.

"You can be angry with me all you want," Cian said, back still to Mael. "In truth, I did not expect you to understand."

The words cut deep. "I am not angry with you, Cian. I am angry at the situation. Furthermore, I do not believe they can be compared to us."

"Have you seen Cornelius since you sent him away?" Cian faced him once more. "Have you seen Brandon?"

"Not since I banished Cornelius and told Brandon that I'd sent him away." Mael knew damn well nobody understood why he'd done it, and that wasn't likely to change any time soon.

Cian knelt before the throne. With nothing more than a touch of his hand, he turned Mael's face to him. "Go see him. I think you will be surprised."

"Cornelius has been banished from my court, Cian. Right now, there is little I can do."

"Then I will show you." Cian lifted his hand and a sphere of blue flame began circling in his palm. An image formed within it, Cornelius sitting in a workroom, doing nothing more than staring out a window, lost in thought. No books lay about; no potions were brewing. Time seemed at a standstill.

"He is not the one for Brandon, Cian," Mael argued, despite the image. "Given time, even the boy will learn that the hard way."

The flame flickered out. "Very well." Cian stood and turned, walking out of the throne room and letting the door slam shut behind him.

Chapter Eight

Cian leaned up against the door and closed his eyes. The coolness of the wood did nothing to alleviate the pain within him. For two days, he avoided Mael, giving them both the space and time they needed. Without Mael's presence, even the tower felt strange, as if something vital had been missing. Cian knew lovers went through this; he'd gone through it so many ages ago with Richard. Yet with Mael, it hurt more than Cian thought possible. Taking a deep breath to steady himself, he opened the door to Mael's office slowly, unsure of what sort of reception he would receive from the prince. It was he, after all, who had walked away.

Seated at his desk, Mael worked, not even bothering to look up. Only the slightest pause in his writing told Cian that Mael knew he was even there. Cian closed the door and found himself unable to move, fearful above all else that Mael would want nothing to do with him. "I'm sorry."

"For what?" Mael asked quietly without glancing up.

"For everything." Cian sat down finally, resting his forearms on his knees. "Mael, please. Just look at me."

"There is no reason to apologize to me, Cian." Mael set the pen down and looked up. "You believe as you do and there's no reason for you to change that. The same holds true for me."

"I know you fear for him, but this is Brandon's choice," Cian said as he stood and walked over to Mael. He turned the prince's chair around and knelt before him. "But I did not come in here to discuss that. I came in here because I love you more than life itself. To know that a rift lies between us is more painful than anything I've ever known."

"And I understand how you feel, Cian. I'm not angry because you feel the way you do. I don't think I'm angry at all." Smiling faintly, Mael reached out, fingers twining in Cian's hair.

Cian sighed with Mael's touch. "I cannot change the way I am, any more than you can change yourself. It is part of what I am to fight for such things. It is why I am here, before you. I would do anything for you and I'm trying to understand your side of things. I can see love like others can see the world around them. I can feel it like others can feel the wind and the rain." He lifted his hand and slipped his fingers between Mael's, grasping his lover's hand tightly.

"And love can die," Mael argued. "No matter the best intentions of the holders. I've known Cornelius almost all of my life. Can a leopard change its spots? I suppose I am to let things go and find out?"

"Even the strongest steel can be tempered with the right fire. We are proof enough of that."

Mael withdrew his hand, his expression hardening. "You are still trying to convince me that I made the wrong decision. Can you not leave it alone for now?"

"You were the one who stated love can die." Cian stood and went over to the window, staring out into the dark night. "I told you, I did not come in here to argue." He leaned against the window frame, arms crossed. "I only wanted to apologize, and possibly seek reassurance that you still love me."

"I still care for you, Cian. That much hasn't changed."

"I am always here for you to turn to, Mael. No matter how much our opinions differ, I am always here."

Mael's arms slid around his waist, drawing Cian back against the strong body. Cian covered Mael's hand with his own as he leaned his head back against the prince's shoulder.

"I never meant to hurt or anger you, love."

"I know, Cian, I know," Mael murmured, mouth pressed to Cian's hair.

Cian turned around slowly in Mael's arms. Slipping a hand under the prince's chin, he lifted Mael's head to meet his gaze. "We are going to have problems, that much I know." He pressed a soft kiss to Mael's lips and drew back slightly. "But no matter what happens, I love you. I always will, Mael."

"You chose one hell of a vampire to love. Somehow I think you could have done better."

Cian stroked his fingertips over Mael's cheek. "Why do you hide what you really feel from me? I can see within you. I know the pain you're in. Will nothing convince you that you are worth everything to me?"

"I don't question how much I mean to you, my angel. I'm just not sure I'm worth as much to myself."

Cian turned Mael's face back to him, the prince's self-doubt palpable. "I am an angel of God. I am one step below an Archangel, and I was created by Michael himself. If there had been any doubt of your soul, he would not have given our union his blessing, Mael."

"And that guarantees you nothing but the fact that they accept our union, Cian. It also shows they realize I would never do anything to harm you."

Cian couldn't help it. He laughed before pressing a kiss to Mael's lips. "I always said you could exasperate an angel, cariad. Now just shut up and kiss me."

"And you're the only angel I want to exasperate."

"I wouldn't want you any other way, my prince." Cian slid his tongue across Mael's lips, coaxing them open. A small shiver ran through Mael's body, and Cian delved into the warmth of Mael's mouth, troubles forgotten as he lost himself in the prince's kiss. "I need you, Mael," he whispered, breaking the kiss slowly.

"And I could never deny you," Mael answered, already working his own shirt open as the shadows transported them to their room.

Cian brushed Mael's hands away and unbuttoned the prince's shirt himself. He pushed it over Mael's shoulders and, with a shrug from Mael, the shirt fell to the floor. Cian pulled away from Mael's mouth and kissed a slow path over Mael's chin, down his throat. As he sucked Mael's left nipple into his mouth, he unfastened the prince's pants, letting them fall to the floor. Mael growled softly, fingers snagging in Cian's hair, tangling in the curls. The prince shifted, cock nudging Cian's cheek. Cian wrapped his hand around the hard length and rolled his tongue around the head, collecting the sweet drops from the tip. Then he looked up and held Mael's gaze as he swallowed the prince completely.

A sharp hunger stared back at Cian as Mael slowly fucked his mouth. The sound of the prince's growl deepened, and Cian's gaze never wavered. He gripped Mael's hip, pushing and pulling as he began sucking with every thrust. After a few moments, he pulled away, moving back as he stood and tugged his shirt over his head. Cian's hunger for blood and much more took precedence, and he made quick work of his pants and boots. Then he crooked a finger at Mael, beckoning the prince over as he backed up to the bed.

Mael shoved him backward and pinned Cian to the bed, demanding entry into his mouth. Cian opened for him, returning the fevered kiss. He gripped Mael's shoulder and managed to flip them. Straddling the prince, he ground down hard as Mael's cock nestled in the crack of his ass.

Words long gone, Cian jerked the drawer in the bedside table open roughly and found the lube. He moved back far enough to grip Mael's cock, slicking it with the gel before he tossed the closed bottle back into the drawer. Then Cian rose up and sank down, entire body shuddering as Mael's cock filled him.

"Fuck me," he groaned, fingers digging into Mael's chest. Sometimes, this was what he needed: hard, unrelenting, the unforgiving thrusts as Mael took over his body. The muscles of Cian's thighs tightened as he slid up and down on Mael's cock, grinding against the prince. He ran his hands over Mael's chest and twisted both nipples sharply. Every hard stroke of Mael's cock deep inside him drew out another shudder. "Oh fuck... Mael... don't stop..."

"I'm not stopping until you scream for me," Mael rumbled, hips snapping up hard, over and over.

Cian pumped his cock hard and fast, keeping the rhythm, eyes wide. "Mael..."

Without warning, Mael rolled and grabbed Cian's legs, forcing them up and wide apart. Cian shouted, back arching as the position left him at Mael's mercy, strokes deeper and harder.

When Mael's fangs sank into the side of Cian's throat, Cian cried out, tangling his fingers in Mael's hair as he held his lover close. He jerked beneath Mael, every hard thrust sending sparks through him.

The friction over his cock was near painful, and just when he thought he could handle no more, one particular stroke tripped him over the edge. Intense pleasure ripped through Cian's body, drawing violent tremors out of him as every muscle tightened and released.

Mael drank heavily, keeping Cian at the peak over and over again. A split second later, the prince's bite strengthened and heat flooded Cian, Mael rocking into him. Tightening his hold in Mael's hair, Cian pulled Mael from his neck and into a brutal kiss, another hunger quickly rising, overriding everything else at that moment. Mael broke the kiss and tipped his head, a wound opening at the side of his throat. Cian moaned and lapped at the blood, heedless of the mess as it dripped onto his skin. It was a taste he would never tire of, the power and flavor more addictive than any wine. When he had his fill, Cian let his head fall back onto the pillow and he struggled to catch his breath. He released Mael's hair and slid his hands down the prince's back to hold Mael close. Tremors still echoed through him, but they were subdued now.

"Rwy'n dy garu di, my prince."

* * *

When Mael woke, he was alone. He blinked his eyes open and stared up at the canopy over the bed, thoughts in a million different directions. He didn't want to think about the troubles at hand, but there was no way around them. Between the issues with Cornelius and Brandon, and the very real possibility of a traitor in his own court, Mael couldn't help but wish he could just close his eyes and ignore it all. Unfortunately, doing so wouldn't fix anything.

A knock sounded on the door. "Your Excellency?" Jensen's voice trembled, quite unlike the man's usual calm demeanor. Something was wrong. "In the throne room…"

Something was very wrong. Mael got up and dressed quickly. When he opened the bedroom door, Jensen was gone. Mael hurried, almost ran, down the stairs. When he reached the throne room doors the scent hit him and sent him reeling.

Blood. Jake's.

He threw open the doors and a chill ran through him. A lump of bloody flesh had been placed on the seat of his throne and he recognized it for what it was: his enforcer's heart. Mael roared, the sound vibrating the air in the empty room. He approached the dais and scowled, the beast inside swelling, demanding revenge. Picking up the still-beating heart, Mael cradled it carefully in his hands. Whirling around, aware of someone behind him, he saw his angel carrying the motionless body of his enforcer. A sense of urgency hit him because he still had time to save Jake. The rage over the invasion of his palace and attack on one of his people had to wait.

"I may still have time," Mael said.

Cian laid Jake's body on the floor. He sat back, watching as Mael worked to save the enforcer's life. "I found him a few blocks away. I didn't see anyone around, but I know who did this, Mael." With a slow, delicate touch, Mael attempted to reinsert the heart into the cavity of Jake's chest. Knowing Jake was probably aware of everything around him and in a great deal of pain, a surge of Mael's power worked to numb the enforcer before Mael withdrew his fingers. Heat radiated from Mael as he tapped into the core of energy needed to heal, drawing on the power in his own blood. A golden glow surrounded his hands as he held them above Jake's chest, passing them slowly back and forth over the wound. In his mind, he saw the fragile threads that needed to be reconnected and he directed the force to work. His energy seeped into his enforcer, keeping Jake quiet as the outer skin began to slowly knit itself closed. Once that was done, Mael continued working within Jake's chest as he sent a thought to his angel.

"Cian, get Jensen. Jake will need some bottles of blood once I'm done, and so will I."

The warmth of energy saturated Jake's flesh. Mael's eyes remained closed as he followed the path of each tendril that surrounded Jake's heart. Barely aware of anything else around him, Mael smiled when he opened his eyes to meet Jake's gaze. Mael reached behind the enforcer's neck to help him sit up so he could drink. Cian was already there with the blood. He opened a bottle for Jake and sat beside him, helping him to sit up as well. He nodded one of the bottles to Mael.

"Drink, Mael. I have him now."

The healing weakened Mael, but he maintained the connection so that Jake could feed. As Cian helped Jake, Mael grabbed the offered bottle and drank quickly, feeling his energy slowly depleting the longer he kept it focused on Jake. Mael's expression reflected a calm he didn't feel. The rage behind it was hidden for the moment. That someone breached the defenses of his palace seemed impossible, but the proof had hit him when he had walked into his throne room. As Jake took another bottle, Mael looked over at Jensen.

"Take Jake to his room and make sure Ben is informed."

Jensen nodded and helped Jake to his feet. As soon as they were out of the room, Cian raised his hand, willing the door closed to give them some privacy.

"This place is too well protected," Mael said as he mentally searched for any breaks within the network of protection that encased his domain. "I can't detect any weaknesses, unless somebody has the power to get through them and then repair the damage."

"I do not think it was an outside job, Mael," Cian said as he stood. He walked over to Mael's throne and shook his head.

Mael fell silent for a moment as he drank. Cian's words echoed his worst fears that it was somebody within his own palace. Yet in his position, he never could afford to show anything but calm. To do otherwise would be a sign of weakness. With Cian, however, he knew he was safe. "I am afraid that it might be."

"Zalael did this," Cian said, returning to Mael and kneeling before him. "He cannot enter this place with two angels standing guard. He had someone else bring the heart. The question is: who?"

Mael ran through the mental list of his court members. There were a few who might fit the bill, though how they would have a connection to a demon was beyond his understanding. Very few of his kind trafficked with demons, and those who did were shunned by everyone else. "I don't know, Cian. There are several I would trust implicitly, but there are some in my court who might be interested in the havoc level alone."

"If there are none who would work directly with a demon, then what about with a First Formula vampire?"

Mael knew the heart was meant as a message to both him and Cian. The demon could strike when and where he wanted. Shaking his head, he sighed. "Memnet is a hated name, though there is an underground society that deals in what he does. The enticement of power gained could lure more than one or two. Particularly to Memnet, since most think that they can bypass the full taint under him."

Cian opened his mouth to say something, but the doors to the throne room opened then, silencing him.

Ben walked up to where they sat on the dais and nodded to both of them before speaking. "I have just received word from Rome, Your Excellency. Valerio was attacked in the halls of the Romanorum itself. Witnesses said they heard his screams, but by the time somebody reached him, Valerio's heart had been torn out of his chest."

"Have they found his heart?" Mael asked quietly.

"No, Your Excellency."

Closing his eyes, Mael tried to sort through the nightmare this had suddenly become. Valerio would be paralyzed for the rest of his existence without his heart. The same fate had been meant for Jake. Only by sheer force of will did Mael control the dismay he felt at Ben's announcement. That Diocourides' fourth-in-command had been attacked, shocked him to the core. Opening his eyes, he said quietly, "Thank you for letting me know, Ben. I want you to have Jake moved to your rooms for the time being." He knew his secretary would obey him, and Ben was one of the few he trusted without question. Ben bowed his head before turning away to follow his orders.

"Who is Valerio?" Cian asked once Ben left.

"He is fourth in the hierarchy under Diocourides. The structure is Diocourides, Nikolai, Drune, and Valerio. He was part of the inner circle that has full access to Diocourides. Cian, without his heart, Valerio will never be able to move again."

Cian sat behind Mael, pulling Mael back to lean against him as he kissed Mael's hair. "If someone that close to Diocourides has been attacked, then it's only a matter of time until Diocourides himself is next on the list."

"Memnet's plan is still far-reaching, and as far as I know, the bastard is still in my territory. I have to find him, Cian, before he goes any further."

Cian nodded and tightened his hold on Mael. "I know."

* * *

Mael knew Brandon hadn't returned to the palace for several nights. Even though Cian had probably taken care of him, Mael worried. Yet another trouble he faced: how to win the young vampire's trust back. Before he could talk himself out of it, he called the shadows to him. As they dissipated, he was left standing in front of the Trinity Hotel, a sort of halfway house run by St. Mary's Cathedral. No one paid him any attention as he entered the lobby and made his way upstairs to the second floor. Digging the key Cian had given him from his pocket, he unlocked the door and let himself in.

"What do you want?" Brandon's voice was tired and scratchy, and he made no move to uncurl from where he sat in a chair, staring out the window at the city below.

"I wanted to talk to you, Brandon."

Brandon turned from the window and stared with bloodshot eyes at Mael. What life had once been there was now gone. "So talk."

Mael remained near the door, not making any attempt to approach Brandon. The last thing he needed was the young man bolting on him. A quiet sigh escaped him before he spoke again. "I know you don't understand why I sent him away, and in a way, I hope you never do. I want you to come home. It's where you belong now."

Brandon's fingers curled around the arms of the chair and he closed his eyes, taking a deep breath. "I lost my home, Mael." He stood abruptly and began pacing. "My heart is broken. My soul is in shreds. And you tell me you want me home?"

"You haven't lost your home. I still very much want you there. You will always have a place with me."

Brandon spun around, the anger and pain intense in those dark eyes. "I had a place, Mael! I had a place with him, by his side! The first time I've ever met someone even remotely like me and he's stripped out of my life."

Nothing Mael could say to that would be understood, or even well-received. He could do nothing more than stare wearily at Brandon as he shook his head. "Are you planning on staying in this hotel for the rest of your existence?"

All the fight seemed to go out of Brandon then and he collapsed onto the bed, shaking his head. "I don't know," he whispered. Fresh tears began to roll down his cheeks, and he closed his eyes, taking a ragged breath. "I'm so fucking lost, Mael."

Taking a chance, Mael slowly approached Brandon. Seeing the young vampire so distraught only made his own heart heavier. Taking a hold of Brandon's hand, Mael drew the young man to his feet. "I'm sorry, Brandon, so sorry. Please come home with me."

Brandon's features were more gaunt closer up; his eyes pale and sunken, his lips dry and pale, almost white. "Okay."

"Will you let me feed you first? And if not from me, then from Seth or another?"

"I haven't fed in a while, couple of nights. I just... haven't cared, really."

Lifting his hand to the back of Brandon's head, Mael drew Brandon toward his throat. "Feed then, and don't stop until you've sated your hunger."

Brandon struck quickly, a soft cry sounding as he bit down, Mael's blood rushing into his mouth. He drank deeply, hands gripping Mael's shoulders tightly, body swaying with every hungry pull. "Oh, God, Mael. You taste like him," he sobbed as he licked the wound closed.

Wincing, Mael said quietly, "I had forgotten his blood would linger in mine after I fed from him. I'm sorry, Brandon."

Resting his head on Mael's shoulder, Brandon just nodded. "It's okay, Mael. I'm sorry, too. Sorry for making you worry." He kissed Mael softly, then pulled away to get his jacket. "How is Cian? I haven't seen him in a couple of days."

Most of the worries Mael had, he kept shielded. "Cian is fine, though he's been as worried about you as I have. No matter what else happens, you still are a part of us."

Brandon slipped his jacket on. "I know that." He looked as if he wanted to say something else, but then shook his head. "I'm ready to go."

Mael pulled him close and darkness rose around both of them, taking them home. As the shadows disappeared, leaving them in Brandon's room, Mael studied Brandon for a moment. "Would you prefer another room? You don't have to stay in this one if you don't want to."

Brandon looked around as if he was in a daze. "No. This is fine." He sighed as he collapsed onto the bed, eyes closed as he swallowed hard. "Just... I just need a while, Mael."

"You can have all the time you want, Brandon." Turning on his heel, Mael left the room, shutting the door behind him. He knew Brandon needed time; they all did.

Chapter Nine

As he stepped into the foyer, Cian froze. Ben and Mael's Son, Christian, were talking, though both glanced over when Cian closed the door behind him. He'd not formally met Mael's Son, but something about Christian seemed... off. Cian couldn't put his finger on it, but he pushed it to the back of his mind for the time being. He nodded when Ben bowed and left, giving Cian and Christian some relative privacy.

"I remember seeing you outside of my Father's private room," Christian said, walking over to where Cian still stood. "You must be Cian Carmichael. I'm Christian Black."

"Yes, I am. Your Father told me about you. Welcome." Cian offered his hand, and Christian's fingers curled around his with a strength that rivaled Mael's.

"He told me some about you as well. I've been wanting to meet you. Anybody who can shake up the halls of my Grandfather's abode is a decent one to me," Christian chuckled, a glint of good humor in his eyes.

Cian smiled, despite his overly cautious reservations. "It was not my intention, but there are some things we cannot control in this world."

"Intention or no, the old man deserves a bit of shaking up now and then. My Father does, too. He occasionally gets a little too stuffy, though. I'm sure you know that by now. Would you like to join me in the study for a drink?"

Cian couldn't help but laugh. "Yes, I would have to agree." In answer to the invitation, he waved toward the study down the hall. "After you."

Christian entered and headed straight for the liquor cabinet. "I know where my Father hides the good stuff. If you haven't yet, get him to drink a couple of glasses one night. You'll enjoy the consequences." Grinning, he crouched down and pressed a hidden button under the ledge of the cabinet. The bottom door opened to reveal a dark bottle and Christian grabbed it.

Cian cocked an eyebrow at him. "Dare I ask?"

"Do you want the full details or just the general gist?" Christian's grin had a mischievous hint to it as he went over to the open bar. He set out two glasses, opened a small jar, and put one sugar cube in each glass. After opening the bottle, he poured a small amount of the greenish liquid into the glasses. He picked up both of them and handed one to Cian.

Cian took the glass and sat down in one of the overstuffed chairs, peering into the green liquid. He'd heard about Absinthe, but had never tasted it. "Now that you've gotten my curiosity up, the full details."

Joining him, Christian settled in a nearby chair. A quick swirl of the glass dissolved the sugar, and he took a small sip of the strong, licorice-flavored drink. "Absinthe makes my Father so mellow that you can do just about anything you want to him. If you keep him plied well enough, you can spend hours..." Christian trailed off at that point, the grin still on his lips.

Cian chuckled softly and took a drink. He closed his eyes and a slight shiver slid through him. The stuff was much stronger than anything he'd ever had before. "Mm," he murmured, "I'll have to remember that."

"I can see why my Father is attracted to you, Cian," Christian said. "You don't mind if I call you Cian, do you?"

Cian shook his head. "Thank you, and Cian is fine."

"I really wasn't sure what to think when I heard about all of this, you know. Most times, Father hasn't had much luck with personal things. I haven't seen any evidence of sorcery, though, so I think Nigel is really off-base on that one."

Cian opened his eyes and looked over at Christian. "Sorcery? They really think I've enchanted the prince?"

"In their eyes, why else would the Prince of London take up with a sorcerer-turned-vampire hunter? Sometimes they just don't figure there might not really be a logical reason." Shrugging, Christian took another sip of his drink.

"I think he and I both tried to figure that one out and we simply gave up." Cian swirled the drink in the glass. "I really must remember this. Beats red wine any day."

"It has a nice little kick to it, which is why I like it. It's the only thing strong enough to affect us. As for my Father, the first thing I noticed was the look in his eyes when he talked about you. It said quite a lot."

"And what look was that?" Cian asked as he downed the rest of his drink. A hard shudder hit him and he closed his eyes.

Christian spoke in a quiet, musing tone. "Something I've never seen in him. He reminded me of a young man in love. Be careful not to drink too much of this stuff at first, by the way."

"No trouble in that," Cian said as he let his head fall back. "One glass is enough, I think." He sighed. "I had a hard time accepting what I felt for Mael, for many reasons. But the more I saw him, the harder it was to deny."

"You love him, don't you?"

"Beyond all doubt. He means the world to me."

"My Father is a lucky man, and I hope you love him enough to stay with him through the worst. He's been disappointed too many times in that, I think."

"There's no danger in that," Cian said quietly. "The most beautiful diamonds come from the darkest of places."

"What about yourself, Cian? I have to admit I'm curious about you. I take it falling in love with my Father gave you a very hard time."

"Yes, it did. I tried to distance myself from him, but considering that I needed to work with him in dealing with the rogues, I didn't have much choice. I am no different than any other man. I just happen to be a sorcerer and a hunter. Nothing more than that."

Christian laughed, the touch of humor wry. "Sorry, Cian, but I have to argue with you. You wouldn't have captured Father's interest if you were like every other man. I've known him for too many years, and it takes more than a pretty face to interest him."

Cian chuckled. "Perhaps because I'm a sorcerer? Or is it that hunter aspect? The old 'opposites attract' argument?"

"Somehow, I doubt that very much. I'm willing to bet there's a great deal more to you than a beautiful face. A hell of a lot more."

"Not enough to entice a vampire prince, I would imagine. Yet somehow it worked out that way."

"Hence why I find myself so very curious about you. Especially since I've figured any rumors about sorcery were untrue."

Cian opened his eyes and stared at Christian for a moment. "I cannot change what I am."

Christian tilted his head slightly and frowned. "I didn't ask you to. I'm only curious, that's all."

"Aside from the rumors surrounding our relationship, what makes me such a subject of everyone's curiosity?"

"I don't know about everybody else's curiosity, only my own, and mine is just on a personal level. Mael is my Father, and while we haven't been intimately close for many years, that doesn't mean I don't care about him."

"I can understand that," Cian said with a slight nod. "I would be the same if I were in your position."

"That's why I wanted the chance to talk to you. So you might understand where I'm coming from better." Standing, Christian approached Cian, offering Cian his hand.

Cian looked up and took Christian's hand. As he stood, he felt himself sway the slightest bit. "Damn." Okay. Strong was an understatement. Not only was the room tilting at weird angles, but Cian felt himself flush, heat thrumming through him. He needed his prince. Now.

Chuckling, Christian slipped his arm around Cian's waist. "Careful there. Your first taste of Absinthe can be a doozy."

"Now you tell me," Cian muttered. "Where is your Father?"

"I'm really sure Father will thank me for this later. I believe he's in the throne room right now."

"Hm, really..." Cian pulled away and started for the throne room. Upon reaching the throne room doors, he pushed them open and stalked toward the dais, intense need beginning to override everything else, including common sense. As soon as he reached the throne, Cian dropped to his knees between Mael's legs, pushing them apart as he licked his lips. He slid his hands up the insides of the prince's thighs and when he reached Mael's crotch, he squeezed his lover's cock through those pants. He barely heard Christian's whisper.

"Father, you might want to tell everybody to go away. We got into the Absinthe."

"Everybody leave now," Mael commanded. His court members hastily scrambled from their places, exiting the room in very quick order.

Cian wasted no time. Within seconds he had Mael's pants open and held Mael's gaze as he swallowed the prince's cock. Mael made no movement to stop him and a sharp hiss of indrawn breath sounded, the prince's fingers twisting in Cian's hair. Cian pulled back and rolled his tongue around the head. Keeping his gaze locked onto Mael's, he drew his tongue up the underside of the shaft and then flicked it quickly over the tip. Mael growled and his fingers tightened, pushing Cian's head downward again. Cian closed his mouth tightly around Mael's cock as he swallowed it. His teeth grazed along the shaft as his tongue flattened to the underside.

"Fuck, you taste so good."

Mael jerked as his other hand landed on the arm of his throne. "Keep talking to me like that and you'll be finding out how good I feel, too."

Cian chuckled, the sound muffled by the cock in his mouth. He moaned softly, causing a vibrating sensation to slide through Mael's shaft. "What? You mean how good it feels when you fuck my mouth? Or how good it feels to have your cock up my ass?"

Mael groaned and gripped Cian's head with both hands, fucking his mouth with quick, hard thrusts. When his body tensed, he came, the bittersweet flood rushing down Cian's throat. Cian groaned and swallowed quickly, and when Mael was spent, Cian slid his mouth off and licked his lips. Mael smiled slowly and gathered shadows around to take them to the bedroom.

* * *

Cian rolled over onto his side and traced his fingers over Mael's chest. He chuckled at Mael's still-ragged breathing. "Did I break you, cariad?"

It took Mael a few moments to gather his scattered senses into something other than complete chaos. "No, my angel, though you're coming damn close."

Cian smiled and then sighed wearily. "Mael, we need to talk."

Sliding his arm beneath Cian, Mael pulled the angel close. "What do you want to talk about?"

"Every angel, every demon, has a true name, one that only they know and God knows. It is up to that being to then share their true name with others as they see fit. To know such a being's true name is to hold power over them. I am no exception. Cian Carmichael is the name I chose when I was sent to Earth."

The topic of conversation had Mael's acute attention since he already understood some of the nature of true names. "I've heard that before, but more along the lines of demons. It holds true to a degree among my kind as well."

Cian shifted and propped himself up on his arm, looking down at Mael. "Should something ever happen to me, I want you to know my true name, Mael. It is Surael."

Mael stared up at his lover. A dark void forming inside him made him shake his head to clear it. It was something he absolutely refused to dwell on. "You've given me the full power of your name over you, Cian."

"I have," Cian said. "Aside from myself, you and Michael are the only beings in existence who know that name. Lee does not even know it."

"You scare me sometimes in how much you trust me."

"I trust you with my existence, Mael. Should something ever happen to me, that name would be the only way to reach me."

"I know you do, and the thought of ever letting you down scares me even more," Mael admitted.

"You would never let me down, love," Cian said with a soft smile. "But there are things in this world that no one can control."

"I already let you down once, Cian," Mael whispered, Cornelius' banishment weighing heavily on his mind. He knew it had been a serious mistake on his part, but he'd refused to listen to Cian, only to find his angel might very well have been right.

"You didn't let me down, Mael. It was a disagreement, and both of us had valid points to make." Cian leaned down and rested his forehead to Mael's. His next words sent a chill through Mael. "I *can* be killed."

Mael growled softly and reached up, cupping the back of Cian's head and pressing a soft kiss to his lips. "But you won't be."

Cian returned the kiss and pulled away slightly. "I know you don't want to talk about this, but it's something you must know. Should I die, I would return to Michael to be reborn."

No, Mael really didn't want to listen at all. Just the simple thought of Cian ever dying brought him too close to that black abyss that resided inside him. In answer, he simply nodded.

"I'm sorry, love, but it's something I had to tell you." Cian kissed him softly. "If I didn't love you, I wouldn't tell you."

"I know, Cian," Mael sighed. "It's not a subject I dwell on, but I know nothing is ever certain."

Cian laughed and swatted him on the chest. "Well, I don't either."

Mael arched an eyebrow. "And that hurt me how?"

Cian rolled his eyes and fell back onto the bed. "Arrogant, stubborn, gorgeous, and a smart ass," he said with a shake of his head. "It's a wonder I keep you in line."

Smiling slowly, Mael rolled on his side, listening to the sound of his angel's laughter. An idea came to him and he silently issued a set of instructions to a few members of his staff. "You really believe you can keep me in line?"

Cian looked over at him. "Do I want to know?"

"As if you can't keep me in line with the tip of your little finger," Mael purred.

Cian sat up then, shifting away and propping himself back on his elbows. "I can do quite a few things to you with my fingers, Your Excellency."

"And if you save that thought for about fifteen minutes, I personally assure that you won't regret it. Though we both need to get dressed for the trip."

"Trip?" Cian's gaze narrowed, but he threw back the sheet and slid out of bed. A few minutes later he had on his leather pants and one of Mael's button-up shirts. "What the hell are you up to this time?"

Mael finally got out of bed to dress as well. When he was done, he held out his hand to Cian. "Come closer and you'll find out."

Cian took his hand, giving him a wry grin. "Something tells me this is going to be interesting."

"It will be, my angel."

Mael pulled Cian in against him and trapped air within the shadows for his angel. By sheer thought alone, he changed their location, and when the shadows dissolved, they were standing outside a small hunting lodge. The canopy of stars stretched above them, and the silver moon shone through the trees. A small basket sat on the ground beside them, and the sound of a brook came from not too far away.

Cian looked around, then back at Mael, smiling slowly. "Interesting setting. I must admit that I'm very intrigued."

"I had hoped you would be. Tonight is ours without interruption." The caretaker had already come and gone, under strict orders to have the cabin open and his ass nowhere in sight. Mael pressed a soft kiss to Cian's lips before he drew away and leaned down to open the basket. Taking out a blanket, he spread it out on the grass before he gestured to Cian to make himself comfortable.

"Romance, Mael?" Cian asked as he sat down. He leaned back, resting on his palms.

Settling onto the blanket beside him, Mael reached into the basket and pulled out a couple of covered bowls, two glasses, and a bottle of wine. They both needed a place to relax outside of the palace. "I wanted to give you a night of just us—no worries, no court, nothing but you and me."

"How did you know to get red wine?"

"I have a very good relationship with little birds." Mael smirked and opened the bottle to pour both of them a glass.

Cian chuckled. "Why do I have a feeling one of them has spiky, brown hair and puppy-dog eyes?"

Mael tried for innocent as he handed Cian one of the glasses. "I have no clue."

"You don't do coy very well, love," Cian laughed as he held his glass up. "A toast?"

"But I've never heard you complain when I'm naughty. And a toast to the most beautiful night I can give you."

Cian's gaze and smile softened as he touched his glass to Mael's. "Cariad, every moment with you is beautiful."

"I should have known you would say that. But some are more beautiful than others." Mael took a drink, watching Cian over the edge of the glass.

Cian sipped on his wine slowly. "And I thought I was the hopeless romantic," he mused. "We're getting mushy."

When he finished, Mael set his glass down and reached for Cian. He positioned Cian so the angel could stretch out, head on Mael's lap. "I have my moments." He opened the lids on the bowls and set them down beside Cian. Taking one of the strawberries, he brought it to Cian's lips. "You are the only one I have ever wanted out here with me."

Cian smiled and slid his tongue out to lick the strawberry. "Then I am honored to be here, my prince."

"This place is meant to be my private sanctuary. Nobody else comes here but me. Whenever you need to get away from the court, you can come here for some peace and quiet." Mael slowly lowered the strawberry into Cian's mouth before reaching for one of the grapes. The quiet sounds of the night around them had a very lulling effect and there wasn't a soul for miles but them. Mael couldn't have wished for anything more right then.

Cian closed his eyes as a soft moan escaped him. "I haven't had a strawberry for quite some time. I had forgotten how good they were."

"I was hoping you had a liking for fruit, a moonlit night, and a naked body beside you."

Cian licked the juice from his lips. "Yes," he whispered. He reached up and slid his fingertips over Mael's mouth. "My beloved prince."

As he pressed a kiss to Cian's fingers, Mael fed his angel a grape. "First dessert, and then the main course."

"Don't you have that backward?" Before Mael could answer, Cian caught his finger in that hot mouth. He rolled his tongue around it, licking the juice from Mael's skin. His eyes slowly darkened as he held Mael's gaze.

"Tonight is it only you and me, my angel. There is no one else in the world." Gently, Mael lifted Cian's head to shift his position and stretch out on his side next to his lover, leaning over Cian and looking down at him.

Cian threaded his fingers through Mael's hair, pulling him down slowly as his eyes closed and his lips parted for a kiss. "I am yours, my prince, every fiber of my being."

"And I am yours. All that I have to give." Mael brushed his lips in a tender kiss against Cian's before his tongue slid between them to take a deeper taste. He ran his hand slowly over the front of Cian's shirt, unfastening the buttons.

Cian moaned softly as their kiss deepened. The very essence of Mael's thoughts embedded themselves within Cian's mind, letting Cian know everything that Mael felt. Mael only pulled away from their kiss to get rid of their clothing. The desperation for the complete connection between them ate at him. As soon as Mael had him undressed, Cian sat up and unbuttoned Mael's shirt, pushing it off of Mael's shoulders. He then made quick work of Mael's pants, tossing them off to land in the grass with the rest of their clothes.

"I need you," he whispered as he knelt before Mael.

Mael leaned, bearing Cian down onto his back, not breaking the kiss this time as his body molded to the length of his angel's. Cian wrapped his arms around Mael's neck, allowing Mael to settle between his legs. A desperate need echoed in the kiss, and Mael ran his hands along Cian's sides to hips, digging his nails slightly into Cian's skin. A slow rock of his body slid their cocks together and sent a shiver of sensation straight through Mael.

A soft gasp escaped Cian and he arched. "Mael..." He trailed his fingers down Mael's spine and finally gripped Mael's hips, body rocking beneath Mael. "I need you... please."

Mael found the lube in the bottom of the basket and popped the top with his thumb to squeeze out a small amount.

He rose up just enough to slick his cock, then he rubbed the head against Cian's hole, loving the way his angel's lips parted, the way the smooth skin of Cian's throat and chest flushed. A slow push opened Cian's body to him, letting Mael take his time to savor the feeling.

"Oh, God..." Cian breathed. His head tilted back, neck arching, as he wrapped his legs around Mael's waist, pulling Mael deeper.

Mael lowered his head to the angel's throat, teeth on Cian's skin as the movement of his hips set a slow, steady pace, each thrust pushing more deeply than the last. Cian moaned, rocking to meet every stroke, the heat of his body enveloping Mael, body and soul. When Cian opened himself fully, Mael felt it, like a wave dragging him deeper until nothing separated them. It was the closest Mael had ever come to this, to being a part of another soul.

"Please." The whisper brushed Mael's ear, Cian baring himself.

Sliding his hand between them, Mael stroked Cian's cock in time with the movement of his hips, driving more quickly into Cian. His mind merging completely with Cian's, Mael sank his fangs into his angel's throat, drinking heavily. With a sudden hard thrust, he buried himself fully, deep shudders slamming into him as he came.

"Mael!" Cian cried out and thrust into Mael's fist, warmth spilling over Mael's fingers.

In that moment of absolute peace, when their natural defenses were down, Mael allowed the shadows to descend over them, blending their bodies. Mael sank even deeper into Cian until no thought was his own and they were one. Cian gasped, and Mael felt the shiver echoing around them. But there was a danger in staying in this form too long: it could become addictive.

"We will always be one, my angel. Always."

When they parted, returning to their own bodies, Cian opened his eyes and looked up at Mael. "I love you." He cupped Mael's face softly and pressed a kiss to Mael's forehead, giving Mael a glimpse of his own magic. White. Pure. So intense and perfect that it took Mael's breath away.

Mael found himself lost again in the life that Cian breathed into him. Cian had made their minds one, he had made their bodies one, and for the first time in all his existence, Mael felt whole. The darkness slowly faded, leaving him where they had been. With the help of his wings, Cian rolled them over until he was straddling Mael. He sat up slowly and closed his eyes. When Cian finally opened them again, their blue depths had faded to white. Without moving from his position, he pulled Mael to sit up.

"Hold on tight," he whispered. His wings folded around them, completely enveloping them. "As you are the dark, I am the light."

Time and space shifted, disorienting Mael completely. When Cian unfolded his wings slowly and the brilliance of the sun shone down on them, Mael simply had no words. Verdant fields and valleys surrounded them, and the blue sky above echoed with the cries of birds through the drifting clouds. A gentle breeze blew around them, whistling through the trees of a nearby forest. Cian looked down at Mael and smiled. Shock held Mael's tongue. The sun. And he wasn't burning.

Cian got up and held out his hand. "Welcome to Michael's court, cariad."

No, he couldn't have. *I'm not allowed here.* Shaking his head in disbelief, Mael rose to his feet. "But how?" Turning, he took in the lushness that surrounded him. The rolling, green hills teemed with a brilliant colored array of flowers, and a soft wind rustled through the towering trees that dotted the land.

Cian stood behind him, snaking both arms around Mael's waist. "If there was no love in your heart, if you were not capable of love, then you wouldn't be here," he whispered softly in Mael's ear.

Leaning back heavily against Cian, Mael closed his eyes, feeling the gentle warmth of the sun on his skin. "I haven't been in the sun in almost two thousand years, Cian. I believe it is more your love than any ability in myself."

Cian kissed Mael's head softly and sat down on the grass, pulling Mael down to straddle his lap. "What were you before you were turned, anyway?"

"The spoiled son of a rich Roman senator. It doesn't seem possible, does it?" Mael laughed, draping his arms over Cian's shoulders.

"You, spoiled? Never." Cian shook his head, a grin breaking through. "Judging by your build, I would have thought you to be some sort of soldier."

"Not within the Roman army, but years after I died there were plenty of battles that had to be fought. I served as my Father's right arm for a time." Mael shrugged. He'd had more than his fair share of that and it hadn't taken him long to lose any taste for it.

Cian lay back in the grass, leaving Mael sitting up. "No sword play? You certainly have the build for it."

Mael caressed his hands over Cian's chest. "Too much sword play is more like it. Though even at my age, I'm not a bit rusty. Thankfully, it's only practice now."

"I'd be lying if I said that the thought of you gripping a sword isn't sexy. It's been several hundred years since I've used one, but like you, I'm not rusty."

"We really will have to practice together some night."

"Yes, I believe we will."

"Considering you're older than me, you've probably had more practice at it. But I'll try to give you a good show." Mael's fingers drifted slowly over the contour of Cian's chest as he studied his angel's face. The sight of golden hair spread out on the green grass was a very enticing one.

"I don't doubt that you would, love. But like I said, it's been several hundred years. I don't know if Father Shepard even has my sword and armor anymore."

"I think we can skip the armor. That's not a period of time I'd care to relive," Mael said dryly. "Though I would love to see if he still has it."

"Yes, I would have to skip the armor. It was gold. But my sword, on the other hand, is safe for you to touch. It is stainless steel, with a silver hilt and a sapphire embedded in the grip. Is Mael your birth name?"

"The birth name I was given was Valerius. It's not one I use anymore."

"Does Valerius have any sort of meaning behind it? Or was it a family name?

"Valerius Germanicus Magnus, to be precise. Valerius was my given name, and it means 'to be strong'. Magnus was awarded to me by the Roman senate, but only because I was so damn generous to the city." Slowly, Mael stretched out over Cian, his hands caressing in soft touches the body beneath him. The warmth of the sun above settled deep, giving him a peaceful feeling that mirrored the tranquility of the place.

"You truly are beautiful, prince." Cian slipped one hand back up through Mael's hair and pulled him down for a kiss. The world could wait. The court could wait. This time was for them.

Chapter Ten

Selena stood to Mael's side, leaning over to slide her arm around his shoulders. Aware she was playing with him and nothing more, he simply gave her an amused look when she turned his face so that she could whisper in his ear. Cian's gaze followed her every move, and he tightened his grip on the arms of his chair. He'd become increasingly territorial of Mael, especially when Selena was around, though he knew Mael could hardly fault him for it. Selena's fingers played with a strand of black hair at Mael's shoulder, and she sat on the arm of his throne. Cian's gaze narrowed, knowing Selena was only trying to rile him. It was working. Cian lost his battle and turned a dark glare on her.

"Don't fucking touch him," he said under his breath.

"Selena," Mael warned her.

As her fingers drifted over Mael's shoulder, she asked, "Do you mean here?" Pausing, her fingers caressed down the prince's chest to settle on the front of his pants, gently squeezing his cock. "Or here?" Mael grabbed her hand quickly.

It was only through a sheer force of his will that Cian kept his wings down. Fury roared through him, and he clenched his jaw tightly shut. He could feel the muscles of his wings twitching, daring to come out fully.

Mael eyed her with a repressive look. "Selena, your room."

Cian watched her go, the tension in his body refusing to subside even after the doors closed behind her. "I'm trying not to kill her."

Mael reached for Cian's hand and drew Cian up with him. "You can't let her get to you."

"That is easier said than done, Mael."

"As I don't have the desire to respond to her, there's no real threat."

"You are mine," Cian said, tugging Mael toward their bedroom. "And I'll be damned if I'm going to sit idly by and watch someone else touch you. Especially her."

Once inside, Cian backed up to the bed and draped his arms around Mael's neck, pulling him in for a kiss. Then he released the energy, slowly, a little at a time. He threaded his fingers through Mael's hair, holding Mael as a brilliant light filled the space around them. He kept a tight hold on it, not wanting to overwhelm the prince with the sheer force of it. Mael called it his angel magic, and in essence, that's all it simply was: a measure of magic, of energy, to send breathtaking peace and strength into one's soul.

As the light began to slowly fade, Cian pulled away from Mael's lips. He moved his mouth over Mael's jaw, then lower to lick a slow path along the curve of the prince's neck. He tightened his grip as he drew his tongue over the hollow of Mael's throat, then slowly back up to Mael's mouth. "I need you. I want to taste you."

"Offer yourself to me, my angel. I demand the first taste."

"I am yours." Cian brushed his hair from his neck, baring it to the prince. "Take what you wish." A soft kiss touched Cian's skin before Mael's fangs buried deeply inside him. The pain sent shockwaves through Cian, and every nerve within him felt alive. "Mael," he whispered as he closed his eyes. A shudder ran through him with each demanding pull on his throat.

Without stopping, Mael unfastened Cian's pants, then his hands returned to Cian's hips to push the pants down, nails scraping along Cian's skin. Cian bit at his lower lip, sucking in a sharp breath. With the growing intensity of Mael's feeding, he was amazed he could even remain standing. Every thought but one began to fade from his mind. He needed this. He needed Mael to claim him, more than the prince had already done. The soft press of Mael's tongue sealed the wounds before he lifted his head. Then he shoved Cian back onto the bed. The darkness in the prince's eyes gave way to the beast that lurked beneath the calm veneer.

"Do not hold back from me, Mael."

A deep-seated growl was the only thing that answered Cian, more primitive than human. As Mael's gaze fixated on Cian, he pinned Cian to the bed, his strength keeping Cian immobile, at the beast's mercy. Cian found himself at a loss for words, yet he offered no resistance—only complete submission. This was what he wanted.

"I am yours."

At the same moment his fangs pierced Cian's throat, Mael dug his nails deep into Cian's hips. The strong grip lifted Cian from the bed, and with a hard thrust, Mael buried his cock deeply inside. Cian cried out, arching into Mael, the need to feel overriding all coherent thought. The savage nature lurking beneath the surface of Mael's civility came out fully. As the prince drank, he also consumed the essence of Cian's life. The scent of spilled blood pushed them both higher, every jarring thrust from the prince taking Cian's breath away. The sting of the cuts Mael made reached even deeper, as if the prince was marking him fully. In the finest thread of thought, Cian realized that was what he wanted: for Mael to mark him, leaving no question to whom he belonged. He no longer feared this and he would need the memories when his life would be taken. That much he knew: he was going to die.

As if sensing every one of Cian's thoughts, Mael rested one hand over Cian's heart. The burn was intense, but Mael made no attempt to ease it as he permanently marked Cian as his own. The force of the prince's feeding only slowed when he shuddered violently as he came. The pain seared Cian from the inside out, radiating through his body in a hard rush. Cian lost all control and raked his fingers down Mael's back, bringing blood to the surface, as his orgasm hit full force.

Mael continued to drink, taking long moments before he began to withdraw. The grip he had on Cian's hip eased and Mael slipped his other hand up to Cian's hair, holding his angel close. Cian drew his hands back up Mael's back, healing the scratches he had made. He still trembled from the residual effects, but inside he felt more alive than he ever had before. Cian kissed Mael's shoulder softly, then lifted Mael's head to see his face. He had no words for what had just happened and all he could really do was stare into the prince's eyes.

"I'm so sorry," the prince whispered, forehead coming down to rest on Cian's.

"No." Cian lifted Mael's head again. "Please, look at me." He smiled softly as he caressed Mael's cheek with his fingers. "I wanted this, Mael. I needed it. Had I been a mortal, I wouldn't have encouraged you, but although you can weaken me, you can't kill me like that." He traced Mael's lips with his fingertip. "I love you."

"I've felt your love. I haven't the words for that. But the mark, I can't remove it."

Cian cupped Mael's face, pulling him down. "I don't want it removed." He brushed a kiss to Mael's lips. "And I'd be lying if I said I didn't enjoy it."

Mael glanced down at Cian's chest. The mark glowed with the infusion of power and it made his smile widen. "There will be no doubt in anyone's mind."

Cian wrapped his arms around Mael's neck, stretching beneath him. Everything was sore, but it had been well worth it. "Good. Now I've just got to find a way to mark you," he teased.

* * *

Standing outside on his bedroom balcony, Mael stared up into the night sky. The scattered stars were barely visible because of the full moon and the lights from the palace. He longed to see the blackness of the sky littered with more pinpoints of light than he could count. The moment Christian entered the bedroom, Mael could feel his Son's presence. Christian stood behind him and gave him an affectionate hug.

"Father, do you have time to talk?"

Mael covered Christian's hand with his own, giving it a gentle squeeze. "I do."

"I've missed you," Christian whispered.

Slowly turning to face Christian, Mael quietly studied his Son's face. "The last time you left, you were extremely angry with me, Christian."

"I've been angry with you more times than I can count, but I always came back." Christian circled Mael's neck with his arms and grinned. "Why would the last time make much difference?"

"Christian, you hate how I get. Each time you come back, you end up leaving in a fit of anger again."

"Oh, but while I'm here, it's intensely interesting. You never could curb that possessive tendency of yours, and I'm too damn independent for it. I'm still your Son and I've still missed you. Just as I always do."

As Mael looked into the dark depths of eyes so similar to his own, he saw desire and need. It never changed with Christian. He leaned forward, placing a soft kiss to Christian's forehead. "Things are different now, my Child."

A tinge of hurt flickered briefly in Christian's eyes, then disappeared. "Why? It has never been different before. You've had other lovers and still let me back in. I know Cian loves you and I would never interfere. I never have before, you know that."

It did no good for Christian to hide anything; Mael knew each thought and emotion before it even fully formed in his Son's mind. "I have no desire for any other. Cian is the only one…" Before he could finish, Christian's lips caught his in a desperate kiss. Mael heard the silent echo of his Son's thoughts, tugging in his mind with a needful plea. Before it could go too far, however, Mael gently broke off the kiss. "I am still here for you. I always will be. But not in that way." The door opened, inviting a situation Mael never wanted to happen.

"Mael, I…" Cian froze in the doorway and stared at the two of them.

Shaking his head, Mael reached out mentally. "I will explain in a moment." A surge of Mael's power entered Christian, pulling him into a deep sleep as Mael carefully picked him up, cradling his Son in his arms. Darkness enshrouded both of them and Mael stepped into Christian's room. He placed Christian on the bed, then returned to his bedroom.

Cian was standing on the balcony, head bowed. Mael knew Cian didn't understand, but it didn't help the hurt and distress too see what Cian had seen. Mael drew Cian back up against him and kissed the golden hair.

"It's not what you think. It's a hell of a lot more complicated."

"That wasn't a sight I ever wanted to see," Cian said quietly. "Please explain it to me, Mael."

"Look at me, Cian, please." Mael loosened his hold, and Cian turned around to face him. Mael brushed his fingers over Cian's cheek. "Nothing is going on between us, Cian. It never will again. I've already explained that to Christian. For him, it was something that needed to be explained. He didn't realize the change in our relationship."

Cian sighed and looked at a point over Mael's shoulder. "Then please explain your relationship to me. I know nothing about all of this," he said, waving his hand around.

"Christian is my Child. I told you before that he had problems with my nature. Over the centuries, he has drifted back and forth, in and out of my life, when he's wanted or needed me. But always, after a time, he would take off and go back to his own life. He's always known he has a place here with me, and I've never denied him that. I'm his Father.

I've never denied him anything he's wanted. It's the nature of a relationship between our progeny, except most are more accepting of their creator's possessive natures."

"I'm trying to understand, Mael. Please know that. I just..." Cian trailed off and closed his eyes. "I can't share you, Mael. I love you too much. Yes, I'm possessive of you; there is no way I can deny it. To see anyone else touch you in such a way... It eats at me."

"I'm not asking you to share me at all, Cian. That's why I told Christian it had to stop. When things are too rough or he's scared, he will come to me, just as he did this time, but our relationship has changed. I promise you."

"Then you understand what I feel?" Cian opened his eyes and met Mael's gaze. "Because I'm trying desperately to understand your point of view. In some ways, I suppose the same could be said about me and Brandon."

"I very much understand what you feel." Mael smiled slowly as he kissed Cian before drawing back. "What you saw was me trying to comfort my Child. That's something I could never deny him, no more than you could turn away Brandon for coming to you. When Children age, most things they learn to handle themselves, but sometimes, things happen that are beyond what they can cope with. That is when Christian always seeks me out."

"I know that. I might not have had a childhood, but I do know that much. Having Brandon in my life has helped me to understand."

"Then you understand my own feelings toward Christian. I have no desire to be with him anymore, in such intimate respects. For him, that is hard to swallow. I know he's going to see it as if I'm no longer going to be here for him. I need to get it through to him that it isn't true. I always will be here for him."

"I do," Cian said. "It's part of why I love you so much—your devotion."

"That's a relief. I wasn't sure if I could get through to you either," Mael laughed. "I can no more stop being his Father than I could let you go."

"You should know better than that, Mael," Cian said, lifting an eyebrow. "And I would never ask you to change who you are."

"I've had a lot on my mind and it's scrambled my brain." It sounded as good an excuse as any.

"Well, at least I'm not to blame for doing it this time." Cian pulled Mael's hand down and kissed his fingertips.

"I could use some really serious relaxation."

Cian smirked. "That will have to wait. I have to go see Lee."

* * *

After Cian left, Mael headed downstairs and out to the garden. The realization of being unable to give Cian what he wanted made Mael feel more than hypocritical. The need for Cian in his life was undeniably strong, but love? If anything, the word itself confused Mael. Settling on the edge of the fountain, Mael trailed his fingers through the water pooling at the base and sighed. Lately, peace proved to be an elusive thing. His worries over Christian were only increasing, as was his guilt over Cornelius' banishment. He swore he'd done the right thing. Now, he wasn't so sure.

In his heart, Mael knew what his angel wanted: to know that Mael loved him. Why was such a thing so hard to say? Not for the first time, Mael searched deeply within himself. His own feelings toward Cian were strong, yet confused. He couldn't imagine life without the angel, but how much of his own heart was involved? Did he even still have a heart to touch? Knowing what Cian wanted from him only made Mael feel a worse hypocrite for banishing Cornelius. It mattered little whether his mage could fully commit to Brandon or not, and Mael realized he was the last person who could make that decision when he couldn't give Cian what the man wanted most.

Mael had been watching Brandon since the young man returned home. He could detect no real indication of the vibrant personality he had welcomed into his own palace months ago. The boy was dying inside, and what moved through the corridors now was nothing more than a shell, forced to exist. Sighing, Mael rubbed his temples. He banished his own magician for something he was guilty of himself. Yet he hadn't seen it that way when he'd sent Cornelius away. The belief in wanting to spare Brandon deeper pain still held true, but Mael knew everything would have to be worked out between the two of them. Just as he and Cian had to do the same. He had to find Cornelius.

Stepping into the shadows, it took no more than a moment for Mael to emerge from the other side, into Cornelius' personal estate away from the palace. The mage's workroom was eerily quiet and the sight that greeted Mael stunned him. The magician neither looked at him nor acknowledged his presence. Instead of the usual robes of his profession, Cornelius wore only a sweat shirt and a tattered pair of jeans. Everything that normally animated him to an almost frenetic level appeared completely dead. None of the books, strewn haphazardly around the room, had been touched—each one still covered in dust. There were no potions brewing. The mage simply sat in his chair, staring vacantly into space.

Mael hadn't meant to do this to his friend. "Cornelius." Mael rested his hand on the magician's shoulder. Cornelius glanced up, his green eyes void of any joy. Mael felt no emotion, not even so much as a hint of anger. In their entire relationship, he had never seen his friend like this. "Forgive me, Cornelius. It's time to come home." The moment the words left his mouth, a rush of chaotic emotion hit him full force, anger and despair and relief all colliding inside of him, all coming from Cornelius. Closing his eyes, Mael tightened his grip on Cornelius' shoulder. "I didn't understand. I'm so sorry."

"Just take me to him, Mael."

In answer, the shadows drew quickly around them and when the darkness dissolved, they were left standing at the door of Cornelius' workroom in Mael's palace. "I know now you need him as much as he needs you," Mael said. "Whatever happens, it is for you two to decide. I was wrong for interfering and I will not do so again."

Mael walked down the silent corridor, heading downstairs for the library. It'd taken quite a bit for him to admit he'd been wrong. Acknowledging the pain of being unable to give his angel something that that he knew Cian wanted had been worse. He paused in the doorway, looking into the room, and saw Cian at the table, reading. Mael went to his angel, resting his hands on Cian's shoulders.

Cian closed his book and leaned back with a sigh. "Penny for your thoughts, love." He lifted Mael's hand and kissed it softly.

Slipping around him, Mael sat on the edge of the desk. "How about: I was completely wrong and I've fixed it."

"About Cornelius and Brandon? What changed your mind?"

"It isn't my place to judge what Cornelius might be able to give or not give Brandon. It makes me a hypocrite. You remain with me, even though everything isn't exactly what you want."

Cian laced his fingers through Mael's and squeezed gently. "I remain with you because I love you, Mael. You mean more to me than anything on Earth or in Heaven. You realize that, don't you?"

Mael leaned forward and pressed a light kiss to Cian's forehead. "Sometimes I question your sanity."

Cian chuckled and stood up. He slid his arms around Mael's neck. "Thank you, Mael."

"And what are you thanking me for?"

"For everything. I can see parts of your soul that I don't think even you are aware of. With every day that goes by, I fall in love again."

Mael knew Cian believed in him a hell of a lot more than he believed in himself, and in a way, it gave him hope.

Cian cocked his head slightly. "You still look pensive, cariad."

"Thinking about you and me, and Brandon and Cornelius. When I found him... " Mael trailed off, trying to find the words. "I've never seen him so lifeless. I had no clue that, for the first time, things were different for him."

"Comparing them to us?"

"I hadn't realized, Cian. I really hadn't. He's never been so involved that it interfered with his magic. Magic always came first with him."

"I never thought a vampire could become suicidal, but Brandon proved me wrong," Cian said.

"I think it will be a while before both of them forgive me." Turning toward the door, Mael snaked his arm around Cian's waist.

"Give them some time, love." Cian stopped and turned Mael around to face him. "You really are a beautiful man, Mael. And I adore every part of you."

"So says my angel. Have I told you lately just how much I adore you? If I haven't, you'll just have to keep reminding me."

"How about you just show me?" A slow smile crept across Cian's lips as his hand drifted down to settle over Mael's lower back, pulling their bodies together.

"Now that requires our bedroom for a full display," Mael murmured.

"So what are we waiting for?"

Chapter Eleven

Brandon no longer knew how many nights had passed. His heart and soul had been ripped away from him and now he simply ceased to care. He buried his fingers in his hair as he rested his elbows on the tabletop. Maybe if he got the ingredients just right, he could concoct a potion powerful enough to put him into an eternal sleep, where only his dreams gave him any respite. Just as the tears began to fall once more, Brandon stilled, sucking in a quick breath. He could sense a presence, yet was terrified it was only his imagination playing tricks on him again.

"Show me a sign. Show me you are not another dream," he whispered.

"I'm here, Brandon." Strong arms circled Brandon's waist.

"Oh, my God." Brandon turned slowly around in the mage's arms. "Cornelius."

"I'm home now."

Disbelief warred with elation, and Brandon stroked his fingers down Cornelius' cheeks, a part of him wondering if this was real. He cupped the mage's face softly then slipped his fingers through the raven curls. "I missed you so much."

Cornelius drew in a shaky breath, holding Brandon tightly against him. "I couldn't even begin to tell you how much I missed you."

"I never want to let you go," Brandon said through his tears. "You are my life and my love."

"It will never happen again, I swear to you." Cornelius kissed his head, cheek rubbing over Brandon's hair. "You will be the Child of my blood and soul. I am going to make sure of that, Brandon. No one will ever take you from me again."

"How? I will die before I am ever forced to leave your side again."

"A ritual. You will drink from me, and I am going to drink from you. We will continue until there is no distinction between our blood. I wanted to do this before, but I thought we had all the time in the world. Now I'm not willing to delay it any more."

"I'll do anything."

Cornelius smiled slowly at him. "All I needed was your permission." The shadows gathered around them, engulfing them in darkness. When it dissipated, they were standing beside their bed.

Brandon looked around for a moment and blinked. "I haven't been in here since you left," he said quietly. "I couldn't sleep without feeling you by my side." He gazed up at Cornelius. "If Cian hadn't forced me to feed, I wouldn't have done that either."

"I know it was hard on you, Brandon. I felt every moment. But here is where you belong from now on."

"Always. I want to touch," Brandon whispered. "I want to be touched by you. My dreams haunted me."

"We're going to do all of that and so much more, my Child."

Cornelius released him and began undressing. Brandon brushed the mage's hands away and went to his knees, taking over. With the shirt gone, Brandon ran his hands slowly over Cornelius' chest, relearning the mage's body. He had no idea how long Cornelius had been gone, but it felt like ages. Every curve, every muscle, Brandon touched with hands and mouth, eyes closing as he savored the body before him. He'd been so afraid he'd never see this man again, and every kiss washed the fear away. He stopped long enough to pull his own shirt over his head and toss it to the floor. Then he unfastened his pants, letting them fall as well. He stood and stepped out of them, then hooked a finger in Cornelius' pants and pulled the mage close.

"Kiss me?"

Cornelius leaned slowly forward, the touch of his lips at first gentle. Hand on the back of Brandon's head, the mage deepened the kiss, tongue plundering Brandon's mouth. Brandon whimpered and pressed closer after finally getting rid of the rest of their clothing. He wrapped his arms around Cornelius' neck and rubbed against the mage's body.

"Make me yours, Cornelius," he murmured. "Make it so strong that not even the gods themselves can tear us apart."

Cornelius fell backward onto the bed, pulling Brandon with him, recapturing Brandon's lips in another searing kiss. "This is will be for eternity, Brandon."

Brandon straddled Cornelius and propped himself on his forearms. He licked the mage's lips, savoring the taste. Unable to help himself, he rocked his hips slowly. One of them moaned, but Brandon had no idea who. "There isn't a force in existence that could tear me away from you," he whispered. They belonged together, he knew that in his soul.

Cornelius rolled both of them so that Brandon was beneath him, then he opened the night stand drawer. Pulling out the tube, he uncapped it and squeezed some gel onto his fingers. A heated stare held Brandon's gaze. "You belong to me, Brandon," Cornelius said, stroking himself. "As much as I belong to you. Nothing and no one will ever interfere again."

Brandon parted his legs and bit his lower lip. "I need you inside me, not just my body, but everywhere within me."

Cornelius guided his cock to Brandon's hole and teased the head over it, not quite pushing yet. "I will always be a part of you." With a quick, hard thrust, Cornelius filled him.

"Cornelius!" Brandon arched and grabbed the mage's shoulders, eyes wide. He wrapped his legs around Cornelius' waist, pulling his lover deeper. "Oh, fuck..."

There was no gentleness. For Brandon, this wasn't about gentle. He needed it, needed to feel Cornelius everywhere. Gentleness would come later. One of the mage's hands slid down to Brandon's hip, Cornelius' fingers gripping tightly. Cornelius' mouth crushed Brandon's, the kiss far more demanding than any other kiss they'd ever shared. Brandon could no longer tell where he ended and Cornelius began. He bucked with every thrust, Cornelius taking his breath away. He groaned into Cornelius' mouth, his movements becoming frantic.

Breaking the kiss, Cornelius watched him intently, the emerald eyes a stormy, deep green. The hand at Brandon's hip pushed between them and curled around his cock. Then Cornelius withdrew and slammed back in, sending Brandon over the edge. He shouted and jerked, heat spraying between them, spilling over the hand still drawing out the aftershocks. With a deep growl, Cornelius shuddered hard as he came, Brandon's name whispered in his ear.

"Yes," Brandon whispered breathlessly. "Gods, yes."

Tipping back his head, Cornelius smiled. "You are my life and love. You know that, don't you?"

"With everything I am." Brandon framed the mage's face in his hands. "As you are mine, Cornelius. Always."

"What we are about to do, it can't be undone. Only death can destroy it, and even then, I doubt it would." Cornelius rolled them, putting Brandon on top. Shadows curled around them, shielding them in darkness. Cornelius drew Brandon gently toward his throat. "Drink, and don't stop until I tell you."

Brandon nodded and closed his eyes as he sank his fangs into Cornelius' throat. A soft, keening moan escaped him with the rush of the deliciously familiar blood. In answer, Cornelius brushed a reverent kiss to Brandon's skin before biting down, the sting more welcome and necessary than anything Brandon had ever known. Brandon held tightly to Cornelius, his arms sliding under the mage's shoulders as they remained locked together. Even through their thoughts, he had no words for what they were doing. He let his love and need for Cornelius drift through their connection as they fed.

* * *

Once Selena returned to the palace, she fled to one of the vacant rooms on the top floor. The room, though clean, had not been in use for quite some time, the furniture covered in sheets of dusty white. She huddled in one of the corners, sitting on the cool, wooden floor, her back pressed to the wall. Drawing her knees up, she hugged them to her chest as she hid her face. She should never have gone out. The world was no longer safe, not for her. Her Father was always somewhere, always watching. Selena could still feel the bastard's touch, ghosting over her skin and leaving trails of ice in its wake. Tonight had been too close.

A few moments later, a portal spiraled across the room. Selena lifted her head, blinking through the tears to see Michael step through the portal. He knelt before her, pulling Selena to him without a word. A sob welled up from deep within her and unable to stop, she shook in his arms. Michael scooped her up and carried her over to the bed. Not bothering to pull off the dust-cloth, he put her down gently and stretched out beside her. He kissed her hair softly and stroked his hand down her back.

"You are safe with me," he murmured.

Selena curled in against him, face buried in the fall of golden hair, the Archangel's strength seeping into her. Tears spilled freely down her cheeks. "I'm not going back. Never again."

"When this is over, the only place you're going is with me," Michael said. His voice, although quiet, had a strong protective note to it. "When you're able to tell me, I need to know what happened."

The sound of his voice soothed her, helping her to try to regain some calm. Slowly, the trembling eased and she drew back just enough to see his face. "He saw me, Michael. He knows I'm here." Panic started edging out in her again, causing a rise in the tone of her words even as she tried to fight it.

"Shh." Michael stroked her cheek with the backs of his fingers. "I'm not leaving you again. I spoke with Cian and the prince earlier. They know I'm staying here and they've offered me a room. I'd feel more comfortable to have you with me." He placed a soft kiss on her lips and cupped her face. "How did Memnet see you?"

As the panic started to fade, Selena placed a grateful kiss to the palm of his hand. "Thank you, Michael. I need you here with me. I had to leave the house because I didn't want to call Sagan here. Mael wouldn't care much for that, I don't think. I went to one of the clubs to meet him and Memnet saw me."

Michael lifted her head up to see her eyes. "I don't want you stepping foot out of this house without me. If you must call Sagan, then I will be near you. I don't know if he would come to you if I was right beside you, but rest assured that I will never be far. Did Memnet have anyone with him?"

"Hale and Chris were with him; they're two of my brothers. He also had a very tall, blond-haired man with him. I've never seen the man before, but there was something... I don't know... unholy about him. As for Sagan, somehow I don't think he would mind you being around. He's kind of strange and not like most of his demonic brethren."

"Yes, I know of Sagan. He is most unusual, which is why I'm not overly concerned with you calling him. Next time you call on him, I will leave it up to you as to where you want me." Michael sighed before continuing. "With Zalael awakened, things will become worse. I can sense him moving about on this plane of existence, as can Cian. I think he was the stranger you saw with Memnet."

"I've been feeling a sort of..." She trailed off, not certain how to explain the heavily oppressive air that seemed to be settling over the court at times.

"Yes?" he prodded gently. "Cian's felt a strong disturbance, too, although he cannot pinpoint it."

"It's like something dark is hovering not too far away, and everybody is acting more anxious, though nobody is sure why. I'm not sure I can explain it any better than that."

Michael's brow furrowed. "Memnet and Zalael could not be detected that strongly by Mael's court," he said. "Has anyone in particular been acting strange?"

"Several have been. The mere mention of Memnet's name would cause many to quake in fear. I've heard whispers when no one thinks they're being heard."

"Have you spoken with Mael or Cian about this?"

"No, I haven't. I don't think either of them are very thrilled with me at the moment," Selena grumbled.

"Cian's sense of duty is stronger than any grudge. If you don't feel comfortable speaking with them, then I will."

Though she wasn't exactly thrilled with the idea, she agreed to it. "As you wish, Michael." Content with just having him with her, she wrapped herself tightly inside the safety and comfort that Michael's presence gave her. He kept her enshrouded in the protective folds of his wings, giving her a peace that she long thought she'd never feel.

When she woke a short time later, Selena found Michael watching her. "I have to go talk to Cian, don't I?"

"Yes. But I will be waiting for you." He kissed her softly, then stood, drawing her up with him.

Selena sighed and led the way out and back downstairs. Michael gave her a smile, then headed for her room. Selena grudgingly went down to the parlor, where Ben was straightening up. "Where is Cian?"

"The library, I believe," Ben said. He smiled a bit, more than Selena expected. Maybe not everyone in Mael's court was as unfriendly as she'd thought.

Selena stood at the library door, pondering the possibility of just skipping this whole conversation. Cian Carmichael was the last person she ever really wanted to get into a serious discussion with. The man unnerved her, more than she really wanted to admit. Taking a deep, steadying breath, she opened the door. Cian was sitting at the desk, head down as he wrote. It took a moment for him to say anything.

"Looking for a good read?"

Selena forced her expression into something more like her typical nature and less like she was ready to run screaming into Michael's arms again. "No. Actually, I was looking for you."

Cian stiffened slightly. "Why me?"

With a sly smile that she didn't quite feel, Selena sauntered over to the desk. "Mind if I get comfortable?"

Cian nodded, setting his pen down. He motioned toward one of the chairs and leaned back in his, crossing his arms. "What do you need to talk about?"

As he leaned back, Selena sat on the arm of his chair and draped her arm across his shoulder. "About some of the things I've seen recently. Michael wanted me to discuss them with you."

Cian's disapproval of her seating choice was crystal clear. "What things?"

For a moment, Selena wondered if he would dump her unceremoniously on the floor. At first, she tried resorting to her usual teasing him, but as she spoke, the calm veneer began to slip. "My Father. I saw him, Cian... and he saw me."

Anger flashed in Cian's eyes. "Memnet? Where and when?"

Selena stood abruptly and moved away from him. "Last night. He was with two of my brothers and a man I've never seen. Michael thinks it might have been the demon Zalael."

Cian reached out and gently gripped Selena's hand. "I'm sorry. I'm not angry at you. I'm just... stressed," he said. "Please." He opened his arms, offering himself as a safe haven for her.

Despite the tension normally present between them, Selena couldn't begin to resist. Cian represented the same safety that Michael did, and it allowed her to give in as she sat down on his lap, burying her face against his neck. "I know."

"I'm sorry, Selena. We will get through this—all of us. No matter how crazy you make me, I won't let any harm come to you. You know that, don't you?"

"He saw me, Cian. You don't know what he's like, the things he can do."

"Then tell me. Tell me so I know what we face."

"He knows how to make you hurt until there's nothing left. He takes everything, all joy, anything good, and leaves you with nothing. You can't predict him... not even how much pain he'll give. The only thing you know is that it will be bad. He can steal everything inside. It hurts so much, and there's no way out. I can't go back to that. He'll take me from Michael and I'll never see Michael again. He'll taint me again and Michael won't let me come back."

The whirl of her thoughts were the pinnacles of her fear, and tears slipped down hers cheeks, wetting Cian's hair, as a small tremor ran through her. "His power comes from demons. Even I don't know how much he has. But he can't even hide the source of his power anymore. That's why he always stayed hidden. To look at him is to know, only he's allowing himself to be seen in public now, and I don't know why."

"To instill fear, perhaps?" Cian lifted her head and gazed at her a moment before speaking. "As long as there is life in me, I will protect you, Selena."

As her tears dried, she gave him a smile. "I know."

A minute later, the library door opened. Selena twisted around to see a delicious, young vampire stop dead in his tracks. The look on his face was comical. Cian looked over Selena's shoulder.

"Ah, Brandon. Selena, this is Brandon Davies. Brand, this Selena Kerr."

Not having seen Brandon before, she studied the beautiful new face with interest. Almost purring as she slid from Cian's lap, she slowly approached him, forgetting her troubles in the prospect of a new toy to play with. "Such a pretty one he is, too."

"Selena," Cian said with a subtle warning, "He's taken."

"And that means what?" Giving Cian a questioning look over her shoulder, she blew him a kiss before she looked back at Brandon. "My, you are..." She let her gaze travel over Brandon. "Sweet."

Brandon cast a confused, wide-eyed stare at Cian, then Selena. "Um, hi."

"He belongs to Cornelius, Selena," Cian said again. "In every way imaginable."

Just as Selena started to reach out, a sudden, vaguely pleasant sensation flushed through her body. "All right, all right, Michael," she muttered under her breath.

"Michael?" Brandon asked.

Cian chuckled. "It's how he keeps her in line."

Brandon was so sweet, Selena was very tempted to zing the poor boy. Another jolt hit her, though, and she stepped back, scowling at no one in particular. "Nobody understands, I swear."

"Be good," Cian whispered in her ear, even when she hadn't realized he'd even moved.

"Why? It's so much more fun not to be." Looking back over at Brandon, Selena said, "I haven't seen you around here. I don't suppose you know me, do you?" Pausing, she gave him a smile. "I'm the one who tried to kill Mael, only he killed me instead. Or was it you, Cian? I'm not quite clear on that."

"Yeah," Brandon said quietly. "Cian told me about you."

Cian sighed. "Don't make me remind you what I can do, Selena."

"Will it hurt? If so, then by all means, please do." Before Cian could make good on his threat, she stepped out of reach.

Cian groaned. "I did not kill you. Nor did Mael. It was the sword," he muttered, directing a look at her that clearly said, "Don't tempt me."

"Ah, I killed myself. It's still kind of hazy at times. And I say you're bluffing, angel."

Cian advanced on her, backing her up against a wall. He reached up and with a firm grip on her head, kissed her hard, flooding her with an almost painful brilliance. A muffled gasp escaped her as her body was taken over by the overwhelming rush from Cian's light. A swift but sharp slap to her ass made her jerk, caught between two very irritated angels, even if one did remain unseen. Finally regaining her senses, Selena tore away from Cian, gasping.

"All right, both of you, no fair ganging up on me!" She scowled before whirling on her heel, stalking from the room.

* * *

Cian smirked and turned to Brandon. The young vampire just stood still, his mouth open in shock.

Like clockwork, Mael entered the library. "You two were at it again, weren't you?"

Cian gave the prince his best innocent, angelic smile. "Whatever gave you that idea?"

"The fact that Selena snarled at me when she passed me in the hall, and I come in here and see you. Two very good clues," Mael said dryly. Catching the still-stunned look on Brandon's face, he added, "I take it you were a witness."

"You could say that," Brandon muttered. "Although I'm not entirely sure what just happened."

Cian fought hard to suppress the grin that threatened to escape. "Honestly, Mael," he said, attempting to regain some sort of composure. "She provoked me."

"Join the crowd, Brandon, because I'm never sure either." Pinning a dark gaze on Cian, Mael said, "You provoke each other." Cian half-expected the prince to wag a finger at him.

"Hey now," Cian said with a devilish grin. "It wasn't me this time. She was hitting on Brandon and Michael's warnings went ignored." He shrugged. "So I gave her one of my own."

Brandon burst into laughter. "Is that what it was? Jesus, Cian. She looked like she'd been hit by a coat of glow paint! She lit up like a damn light bulb when you kissed her."

Mael just shook his head. "I probably really don't want to know what happened, do I?"

Brandon was doubled over and almost in tears. "All I know is that's either one hell of a kiss, or it fucking hurts."

"It's a bit of both, actually," Cian said.

"I think I need to keep you two separated." Mael eyed Cian with a great deal of amusement. "Or keep you better occupied. I'm not sure which one of the two."

"Depends on how you plan on keeping an angel occupied, love."

Rolling his eyes, Brandon grabbed his book and stopped at the door. "Hey, Mael, you should have him try that kiss on you. It looked... interesting." With that, he walked out.

As the door closed, Mael pinned Cian with a dark gaze and murmured, "I might have to." The hand holding Cian's pulled him against the prince's body before Mael's mouth captured his in a demanding kiss.

Chapter Twelve

Cian paced back and forth in the office, staring first out the window, then at the notes he'd made in the notepad on Mael's desk. His wings fluttered, agitated as he moved and thought. The time was nearing; he could feel it like a tingling pain somewhere deep inside. But this time was different. They had Memnet—a Master vampire—to deal with as well. Cian paused and leaned over the desk, scanning his notes. He'd fought vampires, but never a Master.

"You seem especially upset, my angel. Care to tell me what's on your mind, or should I just read it?" Mael asked as he sat on the edge of the desk.

With a sigh, Cian dropped onto the chair, grumbling as he resettled his wings until they draped over the arms. "I've never done this, Mael. Never faced a Master." Looking up, he gave Mael an uneasy smile. "You'd think this would be a walk in the park for me."

Mael's expression softened as he placed his hand on Cian's shoulder, massaging just a bit. "Dealing with Memnet is never a walk in the park. The man has no concept of life in any form being precious, other than his own. Cornelius is holed up in his workroom, working out ideas. As yet, we haven't been able to flush Memnet from his lair, but something tells me it won't be long. Whatever he and his demon have planned, I don't think it will be long before we find out."

"You remember the name I told you?"

"I remember," Mael answered, giving Cian a wary look. "Why?"

"I am not foolish enough to dismiss the gut instincts I have," Cian said. "If something happens to me, Mael, that name will become a lifeline between us. I won't be able to communicate with you if I'm gone, but I will be able to feel you, to hear and watch you. So long as you remember my name, I will be able to return."

"Do you think I am likely to forget you, Cian? It's not a subject I care to think on, let alone discuss at any length, but I will never forget."

Cian studied the lines on Mael's face, lines that hadn't been there just a few months ago. Even though Mael could no longer age visibly, his eyes held more tales of experience than most could ever comprehend. Cian knew the nature of inner demons, having a few of his own. After so long among humans, Cian found himself feeling more like them than he did his heavenly brethren. He stood and cupped the prince's face in his hands and for several minutes he simply stared into Mael's eyes, and deeper still, into the prince's soul.

"I am not worried that you would forget, cariad. I need you, Mael. Now and always. You will be the only thing holding me to this world should something happen."

"Then you'll be stuck here for a very long time, Cian." The prince's smile had a teasing edge to it. "I'm too used to you being around, stubborn pain in the ass that you are."

Cian lifted an eyebrow at that. "I'm stubborn?" He laughed, feeling much more at ease than he had before. "I'll remember that next time you start arguing with me over something pointless."

"I always said you were the perfect match for me." Mael's hands dropped to Cian's hips as the prince continued. "We'll persevere through everything we face. So long as we are together. That much I know."

"For an arrogant prince, you can be quite optimistic."

"I'm fairly sure you've called me much more colorful things." Standing, Mael looped his arm around Cian and he drew his angel toward the door.

"Haven't called you 'Master' yet, in earnest anyway." Cian just grinned as he opened the door, his wings settling back down and fading from sight.

"I suppose I should bestir myself just to see if I can manage that one, shouldn't I?" Mael murmured as he headed down the hall with Cian. Pausing at the bottom of the stairs leading up to the third floor, he gave Cian a bland look.

Licking at his lips, Cian almost purred. "I'd like to see you try, prince."

"You'll be waiting a few hours before you see anything," Mael teased.

"You cruel, cruel man." Cian clicked his tongue as he fell into step behind Mael as they headed up the steps.

"Well, we do have other things to attend to. Besides, the thought of torturing you has its appeal."

"The last time you did that, you ended up on all fours with my cock up your ass," Cian shot back.

As they neared Cornelius' workroom, the door opened before Mael could answer. Cornelius glared at them both and muttered, "For an angel, you think more with your dick than he does."

Cian chuckled. "Did we interrupt something?" Looking around Cornelius' shoulder, he saw Brandon leaning against one of the tables.

Cornelius stepped back and gestured them in with an irritated motion. When the mage was in business mode, he tended to get pissy if everybody but him was sidetracked. Not surprisingly, Brandon was beginning to exhibit some of the same tendencies. For the next several hours, they discussed everything Cornelius and Brandon had researched and spent the time trying to help with the concoction of several new potions.

* * *

A cloudy haze descended over Selena's mind as she slept. It disturbed her sleep, making her shift restlessly before she opened her eyes. Sighing, a touch disgruntled, she turned to her side to drape one arm over the sleeping Archangel beside her. When her gaze rested on him, however, her eyes widened in stark terror. His once beautiful face was now mangled, nearly preventing any sort of recognition. A scream stuck in Selena's throat and she scrambled backward. Blood covered the bed and Michael, spilling from a gaping hole in his chest. One of his wings was shredded, bent and dangling partially over him. The scream finally broke through when she looked into his sightless eyes.

The door flew open, Cornelius and Brandon rushing into the room. A moment later, Sav and Ben crowded in behind them. Selena's screams echoed in the room and she clawed at her skin and gown, desperate to get the blood off. Hands grabbed her, and Selena barely made out a man's face through the torrent of tears.

"Selena!"

She didn't know who shouted her name. All she knew was that Michael—her beloved angel—was dead. Cian suddenly filled her vision as Mael ushered Brandon out of the room.

"He's dead! He's dead!"

Cian pulled her close, his wings unfurling to close around them. "Shh," he murmured. He gripped her head and held her tightly, keeping her from looking at anyone or anything but him. "Who's dead, Selena? What did you see?"

"Michael. Memnet killed him!" Sobbing uncontrollably, Selena clung to Cian, barely coherent as her body shook violently.

* * *

Cian tightened his hold around her. "There's no way I can get to her to bring her out of whatever nightmare she's stuck in," he said quietly, looking at the others.

"But who—" Michael stopped abruptly. "Memnet. She thinks he killed me."

Mael silently motioned Cornelius toward Cian and Selena, then gestured for Sav and Ben to leave so that they could handle this. Both of them quietly left, shutting the door behind them.

Cornelius stepped forward cautiously. "Let me take her, Cian. She's been given a vision, and I can try to clear her sight."

Cian released his hold on her, whispering, "Selena, you're safe. Cornelius is going to help."

Michael remained silent and Cian joined him.

"Are you all right?"

"I don't know." Michael tore his gaze from Selena and faced Cian. "I can't reach her either."

"Cornelius can help her," Cian reassured him.

Off to the side, Cornelius focused on Selena. "Listen to me, Selena. It's not real. What you saw isn't real. Look at me, let me see your eyes."

Cian knew the moment she looked into the mage's emerald eyes. Selena sucked in a sharp breath and she shuddered hard. Cornelius whispered to her, soft enough for only Selena to hear the actual words. Cian watched them, the premonitions getting stronger. If Memnet could torture the mind of a former First Formula vampiress, what could he do to the rest of them?

"She was terrified of whatever it was that she saw," Cian said when he felt Michael shift nervously beside him. "Enough to not realize that it wasn't really you, I think."

Cornelius held her, supporting Selena as a surge of power from the mage flushed through her. His eyes glowed with a luminescence as he quickly worked to erase the power that had given her the vision. It took him no more than a few moments to clear her thoughts of that influence, and Cian felt the relief, thick in the air. Once Cornelius finished, Selena stirred and tried to pull away from him. When she caught sight of Michael, she launched herself at him before anybody could even blink. Michael caught her, burying his face in her hair. His wings quickly folded around them as he waved everyone else away.

Cian turned to Cornelius. "Thank you."

Eyes returning to normal, Cornelius nodded. "My pleasure," the mage said, more subdued than Cian had ever seen him outside of his banishment.

* * *

Her worst nightmare had come to life before her eyes and the terror still lingered as Selena clung to Michael. "I thought you were dead, Michael. I saw you."

"I am here, love. I'm alive and well. I'm so sorry."

Tilting her face up, Michael kissed her. She returned the kiss and hugged him tight. If it had been real, she would never have recovered. She knew that, and with that thought came the understanding of her own feelings toward the Archangel. It was something she never expected to feel. Whispering softly against his lips, she reached up and caressed his cheek.

"I love you, Michael. With all my heart and soul."

Michael stilled and pulled back slowly, meeting her gaze with a soft smile. "Tell me again, because I love you more than life itself, Selena."

Staring up into his eyes, she knew this was right. She belonged with him. "I love you. You are my beloved angel and without you I would die."

"Then tell me you will be my queen when we return home."

"Anything you want. I would do anything for you."

"I have what I want in my arms. And I will never let you go."

* * *

Mael stretched out on the bed, a special little green bottle on the nightstand beside him. His mind was pleasantly occupied as he waited for Cian to return home. The past few nights had been beyond stressful, in varying degrees. Tonight, Mael wanted for them. No court, no troubles, nothing. Just him and his angel. Folding his arms against his chest, he quietly stared up at the velvet hangings draped around the bed, a faint smile playing on his lips when he heard the bedroom open. He glanced over as Cian slipped the jacket off and draped it over the back of a chair. Then Cian walked over to the bed and crawled across it on his hands and knees to give Mael a soft kiss.

"You look..." The angel's gaze traveled over Mael and then drifted to the bedside table. His eyes narrowed and he looked back to Mael's face. "Positively devilish."

Mael snaked his hands beneath Cian's shirt and drew it upward before pulling it off. "I can't imagine why you would think that. You have too many clothes on, and I gave orders that we weren't to be interrupted for the rest of the night."

A slow smile crept across Cian's lips and he pulled away from Mael to stand beside the bed. He toed his boots off before unfastening his pants, shoving them to the floor. As soon as he stepped out of them, he crawled back across the bed and hovered over Mael. "Is that better, Your Excellency?"

"Much better." Mael stretched, barely rubbing their bodies together. "Would you care for a drink, my angel?"

"If you can find an ingenious way of giving it to me." Cian leaned down and circled his tongue slowly around Mael's left nipple, stopping long enough to bite down the slightest bit.

A slow shiver ran through Mael, and he reached for the bottle. Opening it, he took a drink, then rolled them, putting Cian beneath him. A soft sound escaped Cian, and he opened his mouth, tongue darting out to lick Mael's lips. Lips parting, Mael let the Absinthe pour from his mouth to Cian's. Cian swallowed and then deepened their kiss. He pulled away a moment later, licked his lips, and grabbed the bottle, sitting up a little to take a quick swallow for himself.

Mael pinched lightly at Cian's nipple, lowering his head to graze his teeth over the angel's collarbone. Cian groaned and squirmed beneath him, the sensations of flesh on flesh dizzying. "I thought I could get you to agree," Mael murmured.

"I dare say, my prince," Cian said, "that you could get me to do pretty much anything."

Mael chuckled. After so long living among humans, Cian had managed to acquire a bit of a South Welsh accent. When drunk, he rolled the 'r' in Mael's title, the sound sexy as hell. Getting his angel tipsy was going to prove a favorite pastime. Mael, on the other hand, was more used to Absinthe than Cian. Mael let his fingers continue their soft caress over the smooth contours of Cian's muscles.

"You're up to something."

"Me?"

One press of the button on the nearby remote control queued the opening strains of one of Cian's Middle Eastern CDs.

"If I recall correctly, you owe me a dance."

Cian lifted his head just enough to run his tongue over Mael's lips. "As you wish."

Before Mael could capture that mouth, Cian slipped off the bed and his wings unfurled, enveloping his naked body until only his calves and his head were visible. He closed his eyes and tipped his head back, taking several deep breaths. Attention more on the show he knew would come, Mael almost missed the Absinthe bottle. Finally getting a hold of it, he scooted back to the headboard and tipped the bottle up, knowing he was going to need a drink or two to keep himself on the bed.

Following the lilting sound of a sitar, Cian began to move slowly. His eyes remained closed as his body began to sway from the waist up. His wings parted slowly, the soft tips of the feathers caressing his flesh as he moved. It was then that he opened his eyes, pinning a black gaze on Mael as he extended a hand, twisting it slowly and seductively at the wrist, as if beckoning. The slow, serpentine glide of his body followed every note of the music, twisting gently as his hips began moving in a slow figure-eight.

Mael drank in the revealing, sensual movements. Cian danced as if he was born to it, the focus in the angel's eyes breathtaking. As Cian moved to the music, Mael fell deeper into the angel's spell. Oh, Cian had bewitched him, yes, but not as everyone seemed to think.

Cian dropped gracefully to one knee, then brought the other down until he was kneeling. He leaned backward, arching, the line of his body drawing Mael's gaze like nothing else in existence. Golden curls blanketed the floor beneath Cian as his wings cradled him. With his head tilted back, one hand drifted slowly up his body, from his cock to his lips, and his fingers fanned out over his mouth as he sucked the middle one inside. His other hand glided down, tracing a line from his throat to his stomach.

Riveted, Mael swallowed just enough of the liquor to ease the demanding edge of his arousal.

What had started as a dance was now something much more. He knew the instant Cian opened those pale blue eyes. Pushing from the headboard, Mael knelt at the foot of the bed. He told himself it was to get a better view, but the marks his nails left in the bedpost railing attested to something far different.

Cian's eyes drifted closed once more as the finger in his mouth slid in and out slowly. Mael felt the echo as a ghosting stroke over his cock and he growled softly. As Cian rose up before Mael, he leaned forward, drawing the tip of his tongue from the glistening tip of Mael's cock, up Mael's body, to the prince's lips. He lifted one of Mael's hands and sucked two fingers into his mouth, rolling his tongue around them slowly. Then he lowered Mael's hand between his thighs.

"In me."

Mael smiled and circled Cian's hole. Cian moaned and shuddered, thighs parting even more. "Will you beg for me, Cian?" Mael purred, easing two fingers into Cian's body. He twisted his hand, the slow rub of his fingertips playing over the smooth gland.

"Mael, please." Cian's head tipped back as his hips rocked forward and down, grinding him hard against Mael's hand. "More."

Mael added another finger, stretching Cian open. He caught Cian's lips with his own, his tongue parting them to drink in the taste of his angel's mouth. Cian's moan filled Mael, and his angel's hold on him tightened, hips grinding hard against Mael's hand. Thankful that he hadn't had too much to drink, Mael read the signals clearly. He knew what Cian wanted, but he needed to move his angel into a better position. Slowly withdrawing his fingers, Mael pulled Cian onto the bed. He guided Cian onto his back before finally ending the kiss.

"What do you want?" he asked, blindly feeling for the lube in the bedside table, unwilling to look away from the stormy eyes staring into his. He felt Cian's heart racing, the angel's blood pulsing hot and quick through his veins.

"You," Cian groaned, hips lifting.

Mael slicked his hand, then eased two fingers inside Cian. "Have you ever done this?" he whispered, leaning down to kiss Cian's chest. Cian shook his head. "Keep yourself relaxed. I'll take it slow."

Cian closed his eyes, and Mael felt his angel's body relax, the tension fading. "More."

Mael introduced a third finger, gently stretching. Cian moaned and shifted, breathing beginning to quicken. Mael watched with rapt fascination as he spread his fingers, Cian's hole open and beckoning to him. Cian rocked with him, panting softly. Mael curled his fingers enough to slowly begin adding the fourth. Cian gripped the backs of his legs, pulling them up and holding them apart.

"Don't stop..."

"I'm not going to, my angel." The need Mael felt pouring from Cian kept his own anticipation at a high edge as he slowly continued to fuck Cian with his fingers. Finally, he tucked his thumb in as he murmured, "Deep breath now." He waited for a moment, then he pushed his hand into the tight ring of muscles.

Cian's eyes flew open as his body sucked Mael's hand inside. He inhaled sharply and reached down to grip Mael's wrist. "Don't move," he gasped. "Don't move." His chest rose and fell in a maddening rhythm as he fought to catch his breath. His head fell back onto the pillow and he groaned. "Holy fuck..."

Mael remained still, totally rapt in watching Cian. The tightness surrounding his wrist sent a shudder through him as he fought back his own urge to move. With his other hand, Mael reached for Cian's cock, beginning a slow, stroking rhythm. Cian released his legs and fisted his hands in the sheet on the bed, his body arching.

"Oh, God..." Cian thrust up into Mael's fist before grinding hard on Mael's hand. "Mael... Oh fuck, oh fuck..."

Only when Cian began to writhe and push harder did Mael pump his hand back and forth as he twisted it. The intensity that rode Cian influenced him as well, and he had to fight against the surge that swept through him. His fingers tightened around Cian's cock, quickening, as his gaze moved up to his angel's face, deriving a great deal of pleasure out of giving this to Cian.

Within seconds, Cian screamed Mael's name, bucking and jerking hard. Come spilled over Mael's fingers, and Cian's body squeezed his hand and wrist until Mael was sure he would come right then and there. Unable to stop it, Mael growled and forced himself to go slowly as he eased his hand out. After wiping it on the sheet, he settled between Cian's legs, arms shaky as he held himself up when all he wanted was to bury himself as deep inside his lover as he could.

Cian gripped Mael's head tightly, eyes dark. "Fuck. Me." Without giving Mael a chance to respond, Cian shoved his tongue into Mael's mouth. His legs locked around Mael's waist, pulling him down hard and driving Mael's cock deep inside.

Never one to leave his angel wanting, Mael gave Cian everything. He caught Cian's arms and pinned them to the bed, the pressure bruising the pale skin of Cian's wrists. He bit and licked his way down Cian's jaw, toward Cian's throat, fangs scraping. Cian hissed and tipped his head, meeting Mael thrust for thrust.

"Mael... please!"

Tension returned to Mael's body with a vengeance and there was no way in hell he would last long. The thrust of his hips pounded into Cian with the need for his own release, and he shuddered. Fangs bared, he sank them into his angel's throat, drinking in the rich, red flavor as his own orgasm crashed over him. Cian shook beneath him, crying out Mael's name, warmth spreading between their bodies as his angel's ass clamped tight around him.

When they both finally stopped shaking, Cian kissed Mael's shoulder. "I think you fried my brain, love." He stroked his fingertips down Mael's spine. "I love you."

Listening to the quiet voice near his ear, Mael lapped at the wounds on Cian's neck, teasing small trickles out before he healed them. "I'm definitely letting you into the Absinthe more often."

Cian laughed. "Yes, well, I think I've found a new favorite drink. Did you enjoy your dance, Your Excellency?"

Lifting his hand, Mael traced one finger gently along Cian's jaw. "It was perfect."

Chapter Thirteen

"Your Excellency!"

Selena spun around to face Jensen running toward her. Though she no longer held the title of First Formula, Mael's servant still kindly insisted on referring to her in that way. "What is it, Jensen?"

Jensen wrung his hands together in an agitated fashion, a piece of paper mangled between them. "I found a note on the prince's desk. Memnet has Prince Black." His hand shook as he handed it to her.

Fear rose in her heart as she snatched the paper from him. "Where's Cian?"

"I don't know. I couldn't find him, so I came straight to you. We need to go get him. Memnet will kill Mael."

"I don't even know where the Haverhill Warehouse is, Jensen." Growling in frustration, Selena crumpled the note even more.

"I know where it is. It would take no more than thirty minutes to get there."

Without further thought, Selena grabbed his hand and dragged him with her downstairs. It was harder to tell who was in the greater hurry to get out to the garage. Jensen proved to have hairraising skill at driving as he sped through the streets. Each light that stopped him, he cursed at. Selena understood his fear well. There was no telling what Memnet would do to Mael. The best she could do right now was to get Mael out of Memnet's hands. Then she'd call Michael. She definitely couldn't take her Father on alone. When Jensen pulled into a darkened parking lot, her uneasiness increased.

"Look, Jensen, if I don't come out, go back and wait for Cian."

"That won't be necessary, Your Excellency," he said as he reached for her arm. A sudden stabbing pain followed his touch, and she barely had time to notice the drop of blood on her skin before darkness pulled her under.

* * *

"She's starting to come to."

The hated, familiar voice broke through the waves of black as Selena began to regain consciousness. When she opened her eyes, she had to stare to focus before Memnet came into sight. She tried to move, but found herself suspended in tendrils of shadows that refused to release her. The fear spiked inside her, the smile on her former Father's face far from pleasant.

"How you managed to return from the land of the dead is something you must explain to me sometime, Child. But I am glad to have you returned to me."

"I'm not your Child anymore, Memnet!" Selena shot back, fury warring with terror. Why did she come here alone?

"I see your temper hasn't changed any. You need a reminder of things you seem to have forgotten."

With his words, cuts began to appear, crisscrossing over her ivory flesh. Selena hissed as trickles of blood ran down her skin and she fought against the ties that bound her. Pain radiated deep into her from each cut and grew stronger as more gashes appeared. The illusion that hid her wings fell away and they unfurled, silver feathers beating at the air, trying to lift her up. The shadow bindings tightened more painfully on her wrists, keeping her from escaping as slits in her dress sent the material falling to the floor, leaving her naked.

"Well, my Child, what do we have here? New toys for me to play with? Such lovely wings they are." Memnet grabbed the edge of one and his nails sliced across the feathers and the sinew beneath. Selena screamed, the burning pain rippling through her as his other hand brushed over her breast. His fingers stilled to twist her nipple between them as twin jolts of pleasure and pain shot through her body.

"Your Daughter is an angel?" The amused voice came from the darkness nearby before the demon Zalael stepped from the shadows. A sinister, dark blue gaze roamed over Selena, and she shuddered. This was the creature that had killed Cian once. If Zalael could kill an angel... "You have a greater treasure than even you realize, Memnet," the demon said, circling her slowly. "A very valuable treasure."

Memnet glanced over at Zalael. "What do you mean?"

"I didn't know Michael had chosen a consort." With savage pressure, Zalael plunged his fingers into her wing before he twisted the edge outward, bending it to an unnatural angle. Agony bolted through her as she squeezed her eyes shut, trying desperately to hold back her scream.

"Consort? Who in the hell is Michael? And why does he think he has any right to my Daughter?"

Defiantly, Selena lifted her head and stared at Memnet, hatred coiling inside her. "Michael is the one I belong to. Not you, Memnet. It will never again be you!"

A swift, brutal strike hit her face as Memnet's mind bore down on hers. The weight of it flooded her, fragmenting her thoughts into a million different pieces. A scream tore from her throat, lost in the unbearable pain of being mentally ripped apart. Another slash of his hand laid open her body from chest to navel. The tendrils released her, dropping her to the floor. Her wings curled protectively around her as she writhed in pain beneath them.

"I will kill her first."

"No, you won't, Memnet. She's far too precious for that as yet. Only I know how to kill her and I'm not going to tell you how just yet."

* * *

"Mael! You're safe!" Brandon vaulted down the stairs, coming to a skidding stop in front of Mael and Cian as they walked in the door.

"Of course I'm safe." Releasing Cian's hand, Mael asked, "Why did you think I wasn't?"

Brandon started shaking and his face paled. "J-Jensen told Selena... that Memnet had you... said he couldn't find Cian, so he came to her." He paused for a brief second and swallowed hard. "Oh, God... he took her to Memnet..."

The blood drained from Cian's face. "I'm calling Michael."

Rage shot through Mael as he realized the name of the traitor in his own household. "Do you know where they went, Brandon?" Silently, he summoned Cornelius and Ben to him, instructing the mage to bring what he had to use against Memnet. Nodding to Cian, he said, "Summon him quickly."

"Haverhill Warehouse," Brandon said. "Oh, God. What are we going to do?"

"We are going to stop this," Mael said. "You are staying here where it's safe."

"What? I can't stay here!"

"You will." Michael stepped out of the portal Cian had opened. Clad in brilliant silver armor, a painfully familiar sword in hand, the Archangel looked more formidable than all of them put together.

As Ben and Sav came down the stairs, followed by Cornelius, Mael instructed his assassin, "Take Brandon to his room. Nobody gets in or out. I don't care who. If it's not me, Cian, Cornelius, or Michael, you kill them."

Cornelius threw Sav a grateful look before he slipped his arms around Brandon, hugging him tightly. "You'll be safe."

"No, no..." Brandon chanted. "I want to go! Please..."

"No, you need to stay here," Cornelius whispered. "Now go with Sav. Everything will be all right." Cornelius released him to Sav's care and the assassin took the young vampire's hand gently to lead him upstairs.

"Memnet has her at Haverhill Warehouse," Cian told Michael. "Zalael is there as well, I fear."

"I can't trace her and I've never been to that warehouse, so I can't use the shadows to get there," Mael said.

"I can find her." Michael opened a portal and motioned toward it. "This will lead us to the warehouse. We've got to end this now," the Archangel said before disappearing into the swirling gray mass. The others followed.

When they all stepped out, the warehouse towered before them. Michael's grip on his sword tightened and his wings unfurled as a woman's screams broke through the silence. Without looking back, he led the way. Another scream echoed down the corridor and they all hurried, trying to keep silent while still rushing toward what awaited them.

"She will die first before I allow anyone to touch her!" Memnet roared.

Mael took the lead and stopped, peering around a corner. Memnet and Zalael were both there, arguing over the crumpled body between them. "She's there, though she doesn't look good," he whispered.

"Don't piss me off, Memnet. You won't like it, believe me." Zalael smirked at Memnet as he bent down. One hand wrapped to the back of Selena's neck, dragging her upward.

She was healing quickly, and as Memnet looked at her, he smiled. "Now that is handy, isn't it? Just imagine the things I could do—"

"I'll see you in hell first!" Selena broke free of the demon's grip and went right for Memnet. Four of Memnet's fingers struck at Selena's gut, his nails morphing into razor-sharp talons that sliced through her like butter.

"Selena!" Michael's roar echoed through the cavernous room, and before anyone could react, the doors exploded inward. The Archangel brandished his sword, heading directly for Selena and Memnet. Cornelius and Mael were quickly behind him. The second Cian ran through the doorway, a blue fire flared around the perimeter of the room, blocking anyone from leaving.

Zalael spun around and a wide grin spread across his face. "Well, well, looks like an old friend has come to play." Cian's wings beat furiously, fanning a new fire around him as Zalael circled him slowly, sneering. "You do bounce back wonderfully. I shall enjoy watching you die again."

"You must be Michael," Memnet snarled. With a quick glance to Selena, the elder vampire sent her to her knees.

Michael stood over her. "Come and fight for her if you want her that badly."

"She's already mine. She always has been and always will be." Memnet disappeared from view, then reappeared behind Michael, the slash of his talons dragging over Michael's right wing before he faded from view again.

Blood poured down the emerald feathers, and Michael swung around. "Come out and show yourself!"

As Selena struggled to her feet, a brilliant spark hurdled toward her and flames sent her to the floor, screaming. "Does she respond to you that way? She is an excellent fuck, and has the most delightful screams." Memnet's taunting voice filled the room.

Keeping an eye on everything, Mael went to one side, toward Cian and Zalael, as Cornelius circled the other way, heading for Michael and, undoubtedly, Memnet. Writhing shadows snaked across the floor before they swallowed Mael. Just before he left the safety of the shadows, Mael uncapped the vial and a swarming mist of sacred power surrounded Zalael. Before the demon could react, Mael once again disappeared.

Zalael hurled himself at the nearest target: Cian. His clawed hands caught one of Cian's wings and ripped it down the middle. Cian screamed in pain and a moment later, conjured a sphere of blue flame between his hands. He hurled the flame at Zalael, setting the demon on fire. Zalael shrieked as the flesh of his human body fell away, leaving his true form. He fought to ignore the swarm around him as his cloven hooves scraped across the floor, his hands slapping randomly at the flames. Cian let his rage out full force, rushing Zalael and shoving him hard through the wall. Bits of drywall and wood hung broken around the hole, and when the dust settled, Zalael was nowhere to be seen.

Knowing there was nothing he really could do against the creature, Mael returned his attention to Memnet. It pained him to have to leave it to Cian, but he knew his angel could handle it. Across the room, Cornelius waited for Memnet to reappear. Memnet did not disappoint. Enraged, he came into view amid a cloud of energy radiating around him.

"Kill the damn prince first and then take care of the other one!" Memnet ordered.

Lifting his hand, Cornelius quickly took a step toward Memnet. He blew on the dust, and black powder swirled in the air before it settled on Memnet. Taking his chance with Memnet busy trying to regain his bearings, Michael rushed the vampire, raising his sword and bringing it down toward Memnet's body. Light flashed along the blade before it struck, slicing Memnet from one side of his neck, down his middle, to his other hip. Michael ripped his sword from Memnet's body and swung it around, sending Memnet's head tumbling across the floor.

Zalael roared and whirled around, his red eyes blazing with the prince's death in them. Sparks flew from the strikes of his hoofs to the stone as he rushed Mael. Watching the death of Memnet at Michael's hand, Mael didn't see the demon until it was too late. Cian screamed Mael's name and within seconds, put himself between the demon and the prince just as Zalael thrust a dark blade into his back. Mael caught Cian and stumbled backward, hitting the wall.

Michael rushed Zalael and shoved him through another wall, impaling the demon on his sword. Zalael shrieked and hissed, twisting to get free as the sword's magic began dissolving him. When nothing remained but a patch of charred wood, Michael stood, jerking the sword up.

Cian opened his mouth to speak and blood ran from his lips. His eyes, those beloved blue eyes, widened briefly before the light within them began to fade.

"No, Cian, no," Mael whispered as he cradled his angel in his arms. As he watched the signs of life die within Cian's eyes, he went to his knees, tears falling and staining Cian's shirt with more blood. "Stay with me, my love. Please don't leave me."

"His soul has returned home and there he will be reborn," Michael said quietly. "It's time to let him go, Mael. He will return."

"Ti amo, mio angelo," Mael murmured, voice breaking. "Cian, please. I love you. Don't leave me!" Even as Cian's form began to shimmer, Mael tried to hold onto him. Death in his world was too permanent.

As Cian's body faded away, leaving Mael's outstretched arms empty, Michael stepped forward. He lifted Mael's head. "I promise you. He will return to you." A portal opened behind Michael and he looked to Selena. "If you wish to stay with him for a time, then take care of him. You have a throne waiting for you when you return home."

Both Cornelius and Selena helped Mael up before Selena turned to Michael, letting Cornelius take the prince in hand. "I will return to you when I can."

Chapter Thirteen

A month later...

"Mael."

Though he heard Selena, Mael chose to ignore her. He prayed for the darkness of eternal sleep, needed it to lure him away from the dreams and nightmares. The laughter hurt the most, his angel's voice always just out of reach. Blue eyes haunted him—brimming with love one moment, empty and lifeless the next.

Love.

Cian had waited patiently, never losing faith in him. And only when his angel lay dying in his arms did Mael finally understand.

"Mael, your court needs you," Cornelius said.

Let me die.

Someone tugged him up, and only from the firm grip did Mael know it was his mage. Smaller, gentler hands dressed him, and Mael gave up, letting Selena and Cornelius do whatever they pleased. Reassurances that his angel would return to him were losing any weight as the bleakness wore away at the hope he'd been given. A month had passed, and now he no longer cared if the palace fell to the ground around him.

They got him out of bed and down to the throne room. As Mael settled in his throne, the court members around him were unusually subdued. They all kept looking surreptitiously at him, but he barely noticed. The silence was broken by a crack of thunder outside, lightning flickering outside the garden doors. The throne room doors opened then, and a rather nervous-looking servant bowed.

"Your Excellency, you have a visitor."

Mael gave Adams a slight nod. When Adams stepped to the side, a figure entered the room. Judging from the tall, broad shouldered stature, it was a man. Shrouded from head to foot in a dark gray robe, his face was obscured as he started toward the dais, head respectfully bowed, hands tucked into the robe's sleeves. When he reached the dais, he knelt down on one knee, but did not remove the hood.

With barely a movement of his hand, Mael said, "Arise and state your business." The person could be an assassin for all he cared.

"To do so would require an eternity, my prince."

Snapped out of his foul mood, Mael focused fiercely on the man kneeling in front of him. He stood and descended the steps of the dais, disbelieving. His next words were a command. "Stand now and show yourself."

The figure stood slowly and lifted his hands to slide the hood from his head. A crystal blue gaze held Mael's intently. "Do you doubt your own heart now?"

The bleak darkness that had taken Mael over lifted as he stared into those eyes. "No. Nor do I doubt the love it holds for you, my angel." A restless stir ran through the room at the sight of his companion. Many hadn't believed his angel would return. Holding up a hand for silence, Mael said, "I want all of you to get the hell out of here now." Without waiting for them to leave, he grabbed Cian and kissed his lover hard. Barely aware of movement as the others left, he pulled back, resting his forehead against Cian's. "I was lost without you," he whispered.

In the space of those few seconds, the spark of life returned, easing the void that had threatened to take him over.

"As was I, my prince." Cian ran his fingers through Mael's hair and tilted his head back to see his face. "Now you understand the depths of my love for you. For you, I have died. For you, I live again."

There was so much Mael wanted to say, so much he needed to say. "I should have told you before. I should have never doubted this. I love you with everything that I am, Cian. I always will."

Cian smiled. "I know. I have always known. But to hear those words from you, to hear your acceptance of them..." He stroked Mael's cheek with his thumb. "It is beyond anything I have ever imagined. I love you, Mael."

"And if you ever die on me again," Mael swore, "I'm simply going to have to hunt you down wherever you go." Though his tone held a faintly teasing edge, Mael was partially serious. For the time Cian had been gone, he had been deprived of the light that made up his entire world.

"So we're even then?" Cian said, giving Mael a slow, teasing smile. "Heaven is nothing to me without you, Mael. I watched you. I saw the pain you were in. All I wanted was to come home."

"I know you promised to return, but it became hard to hold onto that." Unwilling to wait any longer, Mael summoned the shadows.

"Aye," Cian whispered. "That it was." When the shadows faded, leaving them in their bedroom, he pulled Mael tightly to him as he leaned back against the door. "There is only one catch."

"What?" Mael wasn't sure he gave a damn if it would cost him his soul to have his angel back with him.

Cian brushed his lips across Mael's and whispered, "My blood was purified. I need you to fix that."

Momentarily distracted by the touch of those lips, it took Mael a moment to realize what Cian meant. But first...

Cian groaned, hands settling on Mael's hips as Mael thrust his tongue inside his angel's mouth.

Mael had missed this, and now he was desperate to feel this body in his hands, this mouth on his. He cupped Cian's head and held his lover still, plundering his angel's mouth, leaving no part untasted. He starved for it, the need inside becoming a sweet ache. It was a long moment before he could pull away to let Cian feed. Mael tilted his head and a cut appeared at the side of his throat. With the tip of his tongue, Cian licked a slow path over Mael's neck, shivering against him. When he reached the cut, he closed his mouth over it, whimpering softly as he swallowed.

"Drink deeply, my love, my blood is yours. As is everything I am or will ever be."

When Cian finished, he pressed a soft kiss to Mael's lips before tipping his head to the side. "Please."

Mael sank his fangs deeply into the tender flesh, reeling at the taste of the only blood that could assuage his strong hunger. Cian's blood was far different than any mortal's. In it, Mael felt the angel's strength, the depth of Cian's love for him. Mael bit harder, drawing a cry from the man against him, Cian's fingers digging into his biceps. This wasn't about feeding. Nor was it about sex. It was about need and love so strong, it went soul deep.

A flood of Mael's emotions escaped him to wash completely over his angel. Within the tide, every part of his being bared itself, letting Cian feel the deepest threads of his love. His arms tightened around Cian as he guided them both back toward the bed. After healing the bite marks, Mael drew his head back.

"I need you, Cian. To be inside you every way I can be."

"Yes. Please." Cian made quick work of their clothing and pressed close when nothing but skin separated them. "I want," he murmured on Mael's lips, "to feel you inside me. To feel the rush of release by your hand." He turned and fell back onto the bed, pulling Mael down on top of him.

The glide of skin on skin sent a shiver through Mael, and he ground his hips into Cian. Blue eyes stared up at him, everything laid bare. No more barriers, no more confusion. The intensity hit him in a rush, and without another thought, Mael thrust hard, reclaiming his angel as he captured Cian's lips in a bruising kiss. Cian cried out, the sound muffled, clutching desperately to Mael as his fingers dug into the prince's back. His body arched beneath Mael's, and he wrapped his legs around Mael's waist, pulling Mael deeper.

"Possess me."

With Cian's words, every ounce of power Mael wielded swiftly invaded the angel, leaving nothing untouched as Mael claimed what belonged to him. Cian bucked, pushing into every forceful thrust. Mael worked a hand between them and gripped Cian's cock. Mael was determined to have everything—Cian's pleasure, his pain, his utter devotion.

"You belong to me, Cian. There is nothing inside you that isn't mine." Mael tightened his grip, quickening his strokes as he plunged deeper into Cian's body. "Give me what I want."

Cian's fingers dug sharply into Mael's shoulders and he shuddered hard. "Mael!"

Slick heat spilled over Mael's fist, and Cian's body squeezed his cock until Mael thought he would die. He lowered his head again to lay claim to his angel's blood, his fangs swiftly driving beneath the surface to drink. Releasing his own control, he set a furious pace, thrusting hard into Cian as he came.

Cian's fingers tangled painfully in Mael's hair, holding Mael to his throat. "I am yours and you are mine. The two become one. And I love you dearly, my prince."

Mael knew without a doubt that it was true. They were so indelibly marked in each other, there could be no questioning any of it. Closing his eyes, he slowly relaxed, though he refused to release Cian. That was something he wouldn't be able to do for a long while to come.

* * *

Mael had been exceedingly reluctant to leave Cian sleeping, but he had court business to attend to. Sighing heavily, he settled on his throne, gazing out over the empty room. All was quiet for once, and it gave him a moment of time to reflect. For the first time, thoughts of giving up his position intruded into his mind. He'd never before even entertained the slightest idea of the possibility, but things in his life had changed. He felt the toll of the years. Everything that had happened in the past several months brought those feelings to the forefront. He only wondered if it was something he really wanted, or if he just needed an extended vacation.

The doors opened and Cian entered the room. Mael watched him, knowing there lay the primary reason to give it all up. He'd lost Cian once; he wasn't willing to risk any more. When Cian knelt before him, Mael reached out and tangled his fingers in the golden curls.

"I'm wondering if everything is worth it anymore."

"I don't understand," Cian said quietly. He looked up at Mael, worry etched across his features.

"My court demands so much out of me." Another heavy sigh escaped Mael as his gaze lingered on Cian's face. "Things I no longer have the desire to give. Once it all mattered to me a great deal, but now it doesn't. While you were gone, it didn't matter at all."

"I would never get in the way of your rule, Mael." Cian raised a hand and cupped Mael's face gently. "But I also hate to see you so stressed out, so frustrated dealing with the court. I watched you while I was gone. I wanted so much to make it better."

"I know you wouldn't, and I'm not sure how much heart I have left for all of this. All I wanted was to have you back." Turning his head, Mael pressed a kiss to Cian's palm. "And now it is supposed to be back to business as usual, only I don't know if I want 'the usual' anymore."

Cian gripped Mael's chin firmly but gently, turning Mael to face him. "What do you want, Mael?" He stroked his thumb slowly over Mael's lower lip. "I missed you so much then. Missed your touch, your kiss, your laugh. The way your eyes would grow dark with desire and hunger. I love you so much and I would do anything to see you happy."

"You. You're the only one I want. Nothing else matters now." The situation was one Mael had never dealt with, but it had put everything in his life into perspective. "I couldn't function without you, Cian."

"You have me." Cian rose up on his knees and placed a soft, chaste kiss on Mael's lips. "You've always had me, since that first meeting in the alleyway. I knew then, and there's no doubt now. I am yours. Just as you are mine."

Mael drew Cian onto his lap. "Do I need a break from all of this, Cian? I don't know what to do anymore."

Cian twisted until he was comfortable, draping his legs over one arm of the throne as he slid an arm behind Mael's neck. He kissed Mael's head softly and sighed. "If you want to know my personal and quite biased, opinion..." He nodded. "Yes, I think you do need a break, love. After all that's happened, I think we both do." He reached down with his other hand and threaded his fingers through Mael's, drawing their joined hands to rest just above his heart. Death might have cleansed his blood temporarily, but the mark Mael had made was still there, pulsing steadily, echoing the angel's heartbeat.

Mael smiled, his angel going a long way to setting things right in his mind. "I will arrange it with the Romanorum. It's no easy task getting time off from this job. Some time of our own would help me make a more rational decision on what I truly want to do in the long run."

"If they give you any trouble, you could always threaten them with a pissed-off angel. I'm not pleasant when I'm angry."

Cian pulled back slightly and looked down into Mael's eyes for a moment before speaking again. "Where shall we go, my prince? I will follow you anywhere."

Mael already felt a great deal better than he had when he'd first entered the throne room. Spending time with Cian was the only thing that could clear his mind and let him regain rational thought. "I like the idea of going back to the hunting lodge. Just me and you and romantic picnics under the stars." With his free hand, Mael pulled Cian back in for another kiss. A light nick from the tip of his fang cut his angel's lower lip, and Mael groaned at the taste.

"Can we have strawberries?" Cian murmured, chasing Mael's tongue with his own. "And Absinthe?"

"Anything you want, my angel, anything at all."

"Anything?" Cian asked quietly as he pulled slowly from the kiss. He stroked his fingers down Mael's face, holding Mael's gaze. "Tell me you love me?"

"I love you more than I could ever tell you, Cian."

Cian smiled and stood, then settled back down, straddling Mael's lap to face him. He slid his fingers through Mael's hair and tipped Mael's head back to lick a line over his angel's throat. "Please."

Arms circling Cian's waist, Mael growled softly as he felt the heat of Cian's tongue on his skin. A small wound opened at the side of his throat just as he drove his fangs into Cian's skin. Cian gasped, the shudder running through the angel's body more intoxicating than anything Mael had ever experienced. When Cian began to drink, he rocked against Mael, arousal growing as they both fed. Knowing he couldn't take too much, Mael licked the wounds. He refused to let go of Cian, however, letting his blood feed the near insatiable craving for it. Only when he thought he couldn't handle anymore did he grip Cian's hips to still the movement. It would be a while before they could seek out some privacy to indulge in anything more than this.

Even aroused, Mael couldn't mask the seriousness. He wanted nothing more than to take Cian to bed, where they could spend the evening wrapped around each other, but duty called. "Sometimes saying I love you doesn't seem enough."

"Your soul says much that your voice cannot." Cian placed a soft, soothing kiss to Mael's lips and slid off of his lap. "Shall we get this over with, so we can continue things in private?"

Mael sighed. "I suppose we should."

As if on cue, the throne room doors opened and those in his court began filing in. Though he tried to hide it, Mael wasn't sure how successful he was. His heart really wasn't in the proceedings and his court would eventually sense it if he wasn't careful. One little chink in his armor would spell disaster.

* * *

Reaching over, Cian laced his fingers with Mael's, giving the prince's hand a light squeeze. He knew their troubles weren't over, but he had faith in them. As he watched the others come in, he smiled when he saw Brandon and Cornelius. Brandon had nearly attacked him when he had come back, and now the young vampire was on his way to becoming a mage himself. Cian felt an odd sense of pride. Cornelius and Brandon took their places behind Cian and Mael, and Brandon leaned down to give Cian a quick kiss.

"Have you said anything to him?" Brandon whispered. Cian shot him a quick look and shook his head.

An entourage from Berlin paused at the foot of the dais, and Mael nodded to them politely. "Your Eminence, Princess Millicent sends her greetings," the envoy announced.

"Welcome to London, George. I received Millicent's letter and I'm more than happy to grant her request. Rooms have been set aside for your stay here."

Returning his attention to their guests and away from thoughts best left for later, Cian smiled and nodded his welcome. Just as Cornelius stood behind and to the left of Mael, Brandon stood behind and to the right of Cian. Cian pointedly ignored the teasing grin Brandon continued to give him. If Mael knew what talks had passed between him and Brandon not so long ago, Cian knew he'd never hear the end of it. He hadn't told Mael anything of what he'd thought long and hard about while he was gone.

George seemed pleased by the gesture and said, "Thank you, Your Eminence." As the envoy stepped back with another bow, Mael turned his attention back toward Cian and Brandon.

Cian looked over and met Mael's gaze. He gave the prince his best innocent smile, although from the look in Mael's eyes, he didn't think the prince believed he was as innocent as he tried to appear. Even Michael had been amused at Cian's admission at wanting a son. Heaven only knew how Mael would react.

The rest of the court session went relatively smoothly, most of the members content to laugh and talk and feed. Cian felt the weight of Mael's gaze every time the prince had a moment away from the others. By the time Mael called an end to the session, Cian couldn't decide if he was grateful or if the shakiness was more than just anticipation of getting the prince back into bed.

When they reached the privacy of their bedroom, Mael closed the door, then leaned against it, eyeing Cian warily. "Why do I have the feeling there's something I don't know?"

"Do we have any wine up here?" Cian stooped to rummage through the cabinet by the bed. Part of him was not looking forward to this. For the briefest moment, he wondered if there was a way out of it, thinking maybe he was completely out of his mind.

"I take it this is something that might take me a while to get out of you."

With a sigh, Cian closed the cabinet, wine bottle in hand. Uncorking it, he tipped it back, drinking a lengthy swallow from the bottle itself. "It's more a matter of not knowing how to start."

Pushing away from the door, Mael approached him. "Why not just start by telling me what's on your mind?"

Cian laughed and met Mael halfway, slipping an arm around the prince's waist as he took another drink. "You'll either want to sit down or get drunk. Or both."

"You realize the longer you draw this out, the more curious I become."

"Fuck." Cian released him and pointed to the bed. "Might as well sit down at least. This might come as a shock. It certainly amused Michael to no end."

Mael's fingers snagged the waistband of Cian's pants and pulled him over. As the prince sat down, he drew Cian to stand between his legs. "Should I give you a minute or ten?" Mael chuckled.

Looking down at him, Cian smiled slightly. "I want..." He groaned and slid a hand through his hair, brow furrowing. "Mael, I want a son." There. He'd said it.

Mael's eyes widened slightly. "A son?"

"Yes, a son. Someone who would have ties to both of us. I first realized how much I really wanted this when Cornelius came back. The first time I saw them together after that, I knew I wanted a child. I thought more about it while I was gone." He pulled away and began pacing, taking another swallow of wine. "I know it sounds completely absurd."

It took Mael a moment to answer. "No, not absurd. Do you mean a mortal child? A small child?"

Cian stopped and shook his head quickly. "No. In my time on this earth I have seen more heartache with young men and boys being tossed out of their homes than I care to admit. I want someone we could love together, who would benefit from being in a loving home."

The look Mael gave him was one of relief. "You want to adopt someone then?"

"Yes, I do."

Leaning back on the bed, Mael rested on his elbows. "What about a vampire Child? Would you consider one?"

"I would." Cian sat down on the bed beside him, setting the bottle on the bedside table. "There is only one thing that I want, however, and that is for the Child to have our combined blood within his veins. I want that link. I'd want to be able to know where he was at all times, whether he's safe or if he needed us."

Another long silence followed before Mael spoke again. "I hadn't thought of siring again, Cian. It requires a great deal of consideration."

"I know it would," Cian said. "I am not asking for a decision now, Mael. I only wanted to tell you that it's been on my mind. Brandon laughed so hard, he was in tears."

Smiling a bit, Mael shook his head. "No reason to laugh. Wanting a child is something that hits others occasionally. Whether it be mortal, vampire, or even an angel."

Cian fell back onto the pillows, stretching his legs over Mael's. "I don't think it was so much that, as it was me that he was laughing at. He thinks I am too serious sometimes." He rolled his head slightly and looked down at Mael. "How is it done?"

"First, you have to find a mortal, and the mortal has to be willing. I would need to talk to Diocourides about mixing my blood, the formula, and your blood. Given that it's never been done, there's no telling what the outcome would be."

Sliding his legs down, Cian turned and crawled over to Mael. "Think on it? If you're not comfortable doing it, then we won't."

"Cian, this is something in which you need to consider all of the aspects. If we created a Child, he would be around for a very long time. You also have to consider what sort of mortal you want and watch him for a time."

"What if I told you that I've been watching someone?"

"Do you truly wish for an immortal Child?"

"If he isn't turned, he will die on the streets, Mael. He's been living off of charity, going from one place to the next. He's twenty-two, but there is more age in those eyes than anyone can imagine."

"And you want him for our Son," Mael finished for him. "Cornelius and Diocourides will have a field day with this. Neither of them will be able to resist the chance to merge vampire and angel blood to see what they can come up with. I will consider what you want. For the time being, maybe you should bring the boy here."

Cian leaned forward to kiss Mael softly. "Thank you. Are you sure it's okay to bring him here?"

"Yes, bring him here. I'll have Ben ready one of the rooms for him. You realize we won't be able to contain Cornelius, don't you?"

"Yes, I figured that. It's not every day a mage gets the chance to mix two very different forms of blood. His name is Taylor Reed. He was kicked out of his home for being pagan. His parents were convinced he was a devil worshipper."

"I'm beginning to believe you've been thinking about this for quite a while, my angel. How does Taylor feel about vampires? Does he even know about angels?"

"I've thought about it long enough to know that he's the one, if you decide to go with it," Cian said. "As a pagan, he has many beliefs and is very open-minded. He's known a few vampires in the past, even slept with a few, I think. As for angels, he knew what I was before I could open my mouth."

"Give me a chance to meet and talk with him, and to talk to Cornelius and Diocourides as well."

"Thank you," Cian murmured, pressing a soft, lingering kiss to Mael's fingers as they brushed over his mouth.

"I've learned to trust your judgment. Though I'm still not sure what I am going to do with another Child." Laughing, Mael tapped a finger lightly against Cian's lips.

Catching Mael's hand in his, Cian held the prince's gaze as he sucked two of Mael's fingers into his mouth. "For me, cariad. For us."

"Yes, but vampire Children tend to be different from what you might be used to."

"And I am not?" Cian slid Mael's fingers out of his mouth slowly and moved closer. "If I can handle demons, I can handle vampires."

Arching his brow, Mael gave Cian a knowing look. "You do a marvelous job at handling this vampire, but I have the feeling the combination of you and me might more than a handful."

"And together?" Cian whispered. "Together, we can handle anything, my prince."

ABOUT THE AUTHORS
Shayne:
She writes, she makes shiny things.

Mychael:
Alter ego of Katherine Cook, Mychael focuses on gay erotic romance
stories in many genres. He lives in the eastern US with his family.
https://www.mychaelblack.com
https://www.facebook.com/mblackauthor/